MUSHY STUFF

Guardian Mates: Book One

By Lyra Lorne

Cover Art and Interior Illustrations by Lianne @fantasyspritestudio

Copyedits and Proofreading by YarnWyvern

Copyright © 2025 by Lyra Lorne

www.lyralorne.com

Contents

Knot Without My Mate

A Mushy Stuff Story

For Lianne

For that first illustration of Lydia and Wold. You were hoping for an author to give them a short story. Sorry, not sorry for accidentally turning it into an entire world.

For Mr. Lorne

For pushing me to hit send on the message about the illustration that I couldn't get out of my head. And for encouraging me anytime I felt like I wasn't good enough.

CONTENT WARNING

Mushy Stuff takes place in a fantasy setting, but it takes place in a world that has some darker themes. Please take care of your mental health and read over my list of trigger warnings before reading this book. You can find a full list of trigger warnings for Mushy Stuff and the bonus story, Knot Without My Mate, at www.lyralorne.com.

Chapter 1

I STRETCH AS I wake for the night.

My den is dark, but light still streams in through the exposed roots of the tree that makes up the roof, so I know the sun has not yet set. I do not care for the sun, so I roll over and try to get more sleep; however, my stomach growls in protest.

I huff my irritation and scratch the fur on my stomach.

I suppose now would be a good time to hunt the small beasts with the long ears that hop through my woods. I do find those hoppers very tasty—the ears are a particularly nice treat.

I unfurl my body and climb the roots toward the opening of my den. My claws scrape and tear at the wood as I pull myself out.

The opening is small and well-hidden, but it's also just big enough for my antlers to fit through without getting hung on a root. It is the perfect home to keep me hidden from any humans that stumble into our realm.

These past few moons, humans have been finding their way through thin places and wandering through my woods more frequently. I will have to do something about them before they become too much of a nuisance. Fortunately, they are easy to scare.

Foolish humans, wandering too close to the realm of the Fae. They do not know how closely they court death by those of us that are bound to the land at the borders. We are bound to protect it and nurture it at all costs.

The scent of a hopper draws me from my thoughts. Hoppers are my favorite prey to hunt because they are so fast and agile. It's a challenge to catch them, and keeps my skills honed.

I pause as I scent and locate the hopper, then silently stalk it until I am a short distance away.

A tiny sound, or perhaps a scent, alerts the hopper to my presence. It freezes for a moment, assessing the danger; my muscles coil, ready to strike.

Suddenly it bolts away. I lunge after it. I give chase, but I do not run along the forest floor. My claws dig into tree trunks, and I use each tree to propel myself to the next. In a matter of moments, I am above the hopper.

I leap down, and in one swipe I grab the hopper and swiftly kill it with my claws. I bury my fangs into its belly, tear off a chunk of meat, and chew ravenously. I can feel the heat of its blood as it drips from my mouth onto my chest.

I once would have taken the time to properly skin and clean my kill, but that does not suit me these days. Now I eat like the beast that I am.

I crouch and continue to tear off mouthfuls of hopper until only the head and ears are left. The ears are my favorite part, and I always save them for last. As I'm about to take my next bite, I hear a faint noise, like a voice.

I stand and catch an unusual scent in the air. Something sweet and alluring.

I palm the hopper's head, then climb the nearest tree to get a better view of the area, but I am not able to see anything unusual. I climb down and stalk the scent through my woods.

I must know what it is. I must have it. I feel this need to make it mine; a feeling I have never felt before.

I reach a clearing, and at the edge of the clearing is a human female. How can this be where that scent comes from? I have never known a human to smell like this.

I stalk closer and watch her. I am no more than two strides away from her, but she doesn't notice me.

I quietly climb the tree nearest to her and find a stable limb to crouch on. I use my tail to hold myself to the trunk. Then I watch her as I finish eating the hopper.

She is looking at mushrooms and doing something with a small box that lights up. I have seen these small light boxes on humans before, but I do not know what they are.

She is human. I can scent and see that she is human, but she also has small antlers. How does she have antlers?

She begins talking to the small light box, but no one talks back to her.

I silently jump down to see if I can get a closer look while she is distracted.

I try to take in every detail about her. I watch the way she moves, and the way her hair floats around her.

Her hair is long and wild and free. Most of it is bright blue, but it fades to a warm brown near the root. I did not know that humans could come in these colors. I frown as I study the color. Not very good for camouflage.

I creep a little closer to her; I can almost reach out and touch her.

I can see now that she is wearing a small crown of false flowers and mushrooms. Her antlers seem to be a part of this crown, so they must be false too.

Does she wish to mimic one of my kind so that she can come here unnoticed? She's not doing it very well, she looks nothing like one of us. Humans are witless though; this must be another foolish attempt to enter our world.

As she moves, her long hair shifts, exposing her bare shoulder and neck to me. Her skin is the color of warm brown dirt and looks so soft. I want to stroke my palm along it. Then I notice the soft dark spots on her skin. They look so much like my own green spots but are also so different. My spots are a lighter green than the rest of my skin, but hers are a darker brown than the rest of her skin.

I'm so busy studying her that I don't immediately notice that she is no longer speaking to the light box.

I'm too distracted to notice that every muscle in her body has gone stiff and she is breathing shallowly.

I only notice all of this when she lowers the hand that is holding the light box and slowly begins turning around.

She turns to face me. Her eyes are wide and filled with terror. She stumbles backwards into the light of the clearing.

I step forward, following her.

I tower over her, and I can see the menacing shadow that I cast.

Everything is quiet for a breath, and then she screams.

Chapter 2

It's the weekend, and I am determined to get out and explore my new town. I want to make the most of the time I have before I start my new job.

I moved here two weeks ago from the city; the same city that I have spent my whole life in. I've only known life around the hustle and bustle of a lot of people and cars and buildings. I'm tired of that life, so I'm starting something new.

I'm slowing down and stopping to smell the roses.

I'm going to find my most authentic self here, and I think I have found the perfect place to start.

My very best memories as a child were from before my mom's illness, when we went to the cabin in the mountains for a couple of weeks at the start of summer. Well...okay, it was more of a villa than a cabin. Our Serenity Villa, to be exact. I didn't care about the villa or the shiny appliances or the big televisions like my parents did. I just cared about exploring the woods around me.

I would get up in the morning and wander all day. I found so many exciting things. There was a creek nearby, and I could always find little frogs along the banks.

There were always interesting mushrooms everywhere, just waiting to be discovered. I always brought a camera to take photos of them. I'm sure my mom and dad were annoyed that our cameras ended up filled with pictures of mushrooms, but I just love them. I know everyone thinks it's weird, but I've loved them my whole life. I don't know why; I'm just drawn to them.

I've looked around on all the socials and checked around town, and I think I have found the very best spot to go foraging for mushrooms. I'll have to drive about an hour away, toward the mountains. There's a big forest there and people have reported finding tons of mushrooms.

Most people that forage for mushrooms are finding edible ones to eat, but I'm too afraid to try that. I just enjoy taking pictures of them.

People did mention not to go too far into the woods. They said there is a small creek that I would need to cross to continue going deeper into the woods. They warned me that when I reach it, I need to turn back. People were really adamant that I should not cross that creek, but...I mean... really? I'm not that worried about it. I don't plan to go deep into the woods anyway.

I pack up my phone, a battery power bank and charging cable, some snacks, a bottle of water, and a towel. All of it fits nicely in my favorite sling bag that is shaped like a mushroom. Once I have everything that I need, I lock up my apartment and get on my way.

I'm so excited that I can barely contain it, so I sing along to all my favorite songs to help pass the time while driving. Before I know it, I'm at the parking lot for hikers. My car is the only one here, but that doesn't bother me. I lock it up and head out on the trail.

This forest is one of the most beautiful places I've ever seen. It feels ancient and powerful, and looks mystical. I walk for a while, enjoying how peaceful it is.

I haven't seen any mushrooms yet, so I decide to leave the trail to find them. Safety is important, so I keep the trail in sight and try to follow its path from a distance. As soon as I get away from the trail, the forest comes alive. There are so many small plants. It takes me no time at all to find the first bunch of mushrooms. Then I just keep finding them. As soon as I stand up from taking photos of one, I walk a few feet and there are new ones. The longer I look, the more interesting and beautiful the mushrooms become.

I get completely lost in my excitement, and I take tons of photos and even do a few videos to share on social media. I can't forget to make content for my MsMushyStuff followers. I try to do a live video, but my cell service is terrible out here, so I just stick with things that I can upload later.

A few videos later, I look up and realize there is a creek right in front of me. It must be the creek that everyone warned me about. I look across to the other side. Why was everyone trying to warn me away from here? I probably should have asked questions about it. I shake my head though, because I realize that it doesn't matter what they were trying to warn me away from. Something about this forest just calls to me. I feel almost a physical pull to cross the creek.

I look around, trying to see anything that is obviously a danger. It looks safe to me, so I take off my socks and shoes, roll up my pants, and tiptoe out into the creek. The water is so cool and feels amazing on my feet. I was so distracted by the mushrooms that I didn't realize how tired my feet were getting. I walk around in the creek for a few minutes to relax. Then I finish crossing over to the other side.

I get my towel out of my bag to dry my feet off, and once I put my shoes and socks back on, I look around.

Something feels different about this side of the creek. I can't quite figure out what it is. Everything looks and feels different, but not obviously so. How are they different, yet still the same? That doesn't even make sense. I try to push those thoughts away. I'm letting the people from town get in my head and freak me out. It's just a creek...it's fine.

I notice something ahead of me that looks like a small clearing, so I start walking towards it. I pass all kinds of mushrooms, but I'm too focused on the clearing to stop. I can't wait to see what's there. When I reach the edge of the clearing, I look out into a sunny glade and see so many little flowers. There are mushrooms here too! I start looking around at all of them and realize I don't recognize any of them. It's like it's a whole new world of plants.

I immediately get out my phone and begin taking photos and videos. I lay down on the ground carefully to take a few selfies with flowers and mushrooms around me, then I get back up and continue exploring. I make it all the way across the glade and stop at the edge of it to record a video for my followers.

I switch my phone to selfie mode and find my best angle before I hit record. "Hi, fellow mushy-heads, you will not believe all the mushrooms I've found here! I've never seen mushrooms like these before! There are so many shapes and colors, and all of them growing alongside each other!

It's a perfect mushroom paradise. Oh my gods, what if I'm discovering NEW mushrooms! What if they let me name..." I go quiet as I notice something behind me. It's some type of shadow. I stare into the shadows, but I can't make out anything. I shake the worry off; it's probably just a large bush playing tricks on my eye. I focus back on the camera and pick up where I left off. "What if they let me name some? How amazing would that be? Oh! Maybe we can do a poll, and everyone can weigh in on the names! Then it would be like everyone..." I see movement behind me in the video, and I go still. That was definitely something. I'm facing the clearing, so everything behind me is cloaked in shadows and dim. But I can see a shape there. It's a shape like a man...but not a man...and has antlers. It has glowing yellow eyes that seem to be studying my body.

Oh gods, what is this?

It's a monster.

It's a monster and it's going to eat me.

This can't be real. It can't be real. I try to keep my breathing even, and I slowly start to lower my phone. I turn around to look at it, and oh gods. It's huge. It's so tall that I barely come up to its chest. It has large dark antlers, and fur that looks a lot like moss. But it stands up like a man and has the face of a man. It has menacing looking claws.

Oh gods! It has blood on its hands and arms and smeared all over its mouth and chest.

For a moment I can't move or make any noise, I can't even breathe.

Then I scream as loud as I possibly can.

Chapter 3

IT'S LIKE EVERYTHING IS happening all at once, but I'm seeing all of it in slow motion.

The moment I start screaming, I also turn to run across the clearing. As I'm turning, I see the monster pause as if startled by me. Then I see it reach for me with those long claws, and I take off.

I run as hard and as fast as I can across the glade. I make it across, and then I'm in the woods again. I make a straight line to the creek.

Maybe this is what the people in town were warning me about.

If I make it across the creek, will it be able to follow me? Considering its size, I don't know how the monster hasn't caught me yet, but I refuse to look behind me and risk tripping. The creek is mercifully just ahead, and I push as hard as I can towards it.

I'm a mere two steps away from splashing into the water when I slam into something that feels like a wall. It knocks all the air out of me, and I fall to the ground. I see a glimpse of the sky through the trees and then everything goes dark.

***

Wold

She ran from me.

Of course she did. I expected her to be terrified of me.

I follow her at a slow pace. I could easily catch her and overpower her, but I don't want to scare her more than I already have. And I don't want to hurt her. I just want to see what she does.

Then I realize that she is running for the creek.

The creek is a border between our realms, and sometimes there are thin spots in the magic there. She must have come through a thin spot at the creek, but now it has closed up. She is going to run into a magical wall.

I open my mouth to yell for her to stop, but it has been ages since I last spoke to someone. My voice comes out in a raspy growl. I doubt she heard me, and even if she did, it would have only made her more afraid.

I'm too far away to possibly stop her, all I can do is helplessly watch as she hits the wall and collapses.

I run to her side. She is still breathing, but unconscious. I pick her up and carry her to my cave of mushrooms.

While I carry her, I can practically feel her scent sinking into me. It's like it's becoming a part of me, like she is becoming part of me. I don't understand it.

Once we get to the cave, I lay her on a flat, moss-covered boulder in a darkened chamber of the cave. I keep myself busy, tending to the varieties of mushrooms that I have so carefully cultivated here while I wait for her to wake. I have some mushroom clusters that have grown too large and are ready for division, so I spend my time very carefully dividing them. This type of mushroom is fragile and can fall apart if I am not careful. But I am distracted by this human. I destroy more than one cluster when I stop to check on her due to the little noises she makes in her sleep.

Chapter 4

OH GODS, MY WHOLE body hurts. I crack my eyes open expecting bright sunlight, but wherever I am it is dark and shadowy.

Where am I?

What happened?

I remember the monster from the woods, and I jolt awake. I sit up and try to figure out where I am and where the monster is. I look around at my surroundings, and I'm in some kind of cave. I can hear water running somewhere nearby. I don't see the monster anywhere, but it's dark enough that I can't be sure. I slowly start to stand up.

From the dark corner of the cave, I hear a rough, gravely voice that says, "Female...are you...well?" His voice is almost more growl than words.

I stare wide-eyed at the dark corner. He's staying mostly in the shadows, but I can see the outline of his body. And his glowing yellow eyes. I say, "Y-yes. W-who are you? Where am I?"

He takes a deep breath and growls on his exhale. "I am Wold. This...is...Ilsarius...the Fae Realm." He speaks very slowly and laboriously, as if it's hard for him to speak.

"The Fae Realm?"

"Yes...you crossed over...to our realm. Are you well? I did not...mean to scare you."

"Yes, I think I'm okay. Just a little sore." I pause, and then decide that it's best to be direct and ask any questions that I have. "Are you going to hurt me?"

"No."

"How do I know if I can trust you?" I ask.

He is quiet for a moment, then says, "You do not."

He's had me here unconscious for only the gods know how long. If he had wanted to hurt me, he would have by now. Right?

"What are you going to do with me?"

He stares at me as if he hadn't thought about that yet, and eventually responds, "I do not know."

This makes me nervous. What does he mean he doesn't know? "Am I a prisoner?"

He quickly says, "No. You may leave...whenever you want. We will...need to make a thin place...for you to cross back over to your world though."

"A thin place?"

"Yes, a thin spot...in the magical wall...between our realms."

His speech seems to be getting a little more natural, a little less forced. His voice is still gravely and almost a growl, but the words seem to be coming to him a little easier. I watch him for a minute longer, then ask, "Why is it hard for you to talk?"

He takes another deep breath and growls on this exhale too. "I have not...spoken to...anyone in a long time."

Oh...well that makes me sad. "How long?"

He looks at me and growls, "Decades."

I stare at him in shock. "Decades?! You haven't spoken in that long?"

He continues to look at me and says, "No."

I feel so sorry for him. This poor guy has been alone for decades. It makes me want to give him a huge hug, but then I remind myself that he's a monster, and we don't hug monsters.

"There aren't other...um...people...like you that you can hang out with?"

He tilts his head to the side. "Hang out? Hang what out?"

Right, I guess he wouldn't know slang. "It means to spend time with friends. You don't have anyone you can spend time with?"

"No."

I gape at him. I can't even comprehend not having anyone. When I was so lonely as a little girl, at least I had the house staff to talk to. To have no one to talk to is tragic. Maybe I can stay a day or so and become his friend. Although, I don't even know what he is. Maybe I should figure that out first. "Are you the only one of your kind?"

He snorts. "No. There are others...but we each guard our own territories. I do not interact with them often."

Oh. "What are your people called?"

He says, "We are Guardians."

"What do you guard?"

He gestures around him with a huge hand that is tipped with lethal looking claws. "All of this. Our land. Ilsarius. The fae world."

I'm so confused. I've never heard of Guardians or Ilsarius or a Fae Realm. I mean, I guess I've heard stories of the fae, but they are just fairy tales. Right?

As we've been talking, he's shifted toward me and out of the shadows. I can get a better look at him now. He's just as tall as I thought he was, and he has black antlers that make him seem even taller. His hair is long and flowing...and moss-colored. Intermixed with his hair, there are strands of leafy vines. They seem to writhe and move of their own accord. His skin is a very dark mossy green. His fur is a lighter green and has a texture like moss, and he has patches of it on different parts of his body. There's a big patch on his back that runs over the top of his shoulders. There are also patches of it on his legs and groin. I think he has tiny mushrooms growing in the fur on his shoulders. His hands are different than mine, he has three fingers and a thumb. Each finger is tipped in a deadly looking claw. His feet look like big wolf's paws with huge claws.

I should be terrified of him. He is terrifying. I'm certain he could hurt me or kill me in the blink of an eye. For some reason, I'm just not afraid of him. I don't know why. He didn't hurt me while I was unconscious, and after talking to him, I just don't think he means to hurt me.

I take a step toward him, then I look around and ask again, "So, where are we?"

He glances around and says, "This is my cave of mushrooms."

I look at him confused. "Cave of mushrooms? Why do you call it that?"

He stares at me as if I'm crazy, then says, "Because it's a cave of mushrooms."

"But I don't see—"

He turns and places his palm flat against the wall. Soft, glowing light blooms from where his hand is and spreads across the entire cave. I gasp. This cave is covered in bioluminescent mushrooms. They are everywhere; they grow on the walls and on the floor. He's made a path through the room to not step on any of them.

I look around in wonder; it's the most beautiful thing I've ever seen. "Oh, my gods! It's beautiful! How did...how did you do that?"

He surveys the mushrooms, and I can see his face soften. He's looking at them affectionately. "My magic. I nurture and grow these here."

I walk over to the wall he is standing in front of. He startles a little as I come to stand beside him.

I study the mushrooms on the wall in front of me. I've never seen mushrooms like these before. "It's amazing...Wold. You said your name is Wold, right?"

He nods.

"I'm Lydia. It's nice to meet you, Wold."

Chapter 5

THIS LITTLE FEMALE...I CAN'T figure her out. She isn't afraid of me, so she may be unwell.

She looks around the cave with genuine awe. I watch her as she studies each mushroom. She really seems to love them.

She pulls out her little light box. "Is it okay if I take a picture?"

I look at her light box warily.

She says, "It's just my phone. I won't use flash or anything."

I decide that I can't see how her light box could hurt anything, so I nod to let her know it's okay. She's so excited that I agreed that she squeals. The sound stings my ears, but it's worth the look of happiness on her face. I watch her use the *phone* to take *pictures*. Her face is bright with joy, and she looks very pretty this way.

Why am I thinking about how pretty a human is?

The longer she is in this small cave with me, the more her scent permeates the air. Hers is the only scent I can smell, and I feel like it has sunk into my core. Her scent is a part of me now.

She stops to look at me while I'm standing at the wall. "Can I take a picture of you?"

This makes me anxious, and she notices how uneasy I am.

"It's perfectly safe." She does something on her phone, then she stands in front of me. She's very close to me, probably within arm's reach. She holds the phone up in front of her and it makes a small clicking noise. I'm too busy looking at her to pay much attention to the phone.

"Perfect!" she says as she steps away from me.

She's still looking at something on her phone when she gasps and says, "Oh! You have a tail! I just noticed it in the picture!" She walks around me to get a better look at it. She studies my tail for a minute, and the attention makes me uncomfortable, so my tail loudly thwacks against the floor. I practically groan with embarrassment.

She giggles. "Is that good or bad?"

Before I can respond, she continues, "Can I touch it?"

I just stare at her dumbfounded. She wants to touch me?

She blushes. "Your tail...can I touch your tail?"

I'm still so shocked that I can't reply, so I just nod.

She squats down and pets the tuft of hair on the end of my tail. She's being very soft and gentle, but her touch still makes my tail twitch. Maybe it's *because* her touch is so soft and gentle that it twitches.

She stands back up and goes back to looking at mushrooms, and I watch her as she does.

She surveys the room and says, "It's so beautiful! I can't believe I'm seeing this."

I think for a moment. "Do you want to see more?"

She turns to me and her eyes light up. "There's more?!"

"Yes, come with me." I walk toward the exit of this chamber, and she follows me.

We enter another chamber of the cave, and she gasps as soon as she walks in.

This room has an opening in the ceiling where sunlight comes through. There's a small waterfall that pours through the opening and into the cave. It creates a small pool towards the back of this chamber.

As we walk in, I say, "This is where I keep the mushrooms that like more light."

There are many, many kinds of mushrooms here. The room is full of color from all of them. They range from beautiful with perfect little rounded caps to grotesque looking. There are some that look like almost exactly like eyeballs. There are other clusters that ooze horrible fluids from their deformed caps and smell foul.

Lydia stands in the middle of the cave surveying everything in silent awe. She finally looks at me with huge, rounded eyes. "Wold, this is amazing. You did all of this? You take care of them?"

I rub the back of my neck and reply, "Yes. It is what I do."

"How do you care for them? It doesn't seem like they need watering."

"No, my magic cares for them. It helps them grow strong," I explain.

She's still looking around the room as she says, "This really is beautiful. I've never seen anything like it. I don't even know what to say."

I watch as a tear rolls down her cheek. This startles me. Did I do something to make her upset? I thought this would make her happy.

I say, "Why do you weep?"

She smiles and wipes the tear away. "Sorry, I'm just being emotional. It's so beautiful that it makes me cry."

This concerns me. Humans cry because something is beautiful? There are so many beautiful things in the world.

If all of those make them cry, then how do they continue existing? She must see the concerned look on my face.

She laughs. "Don't worry about it. I'm just crying because this place is so perfect for me. I never could have imagined seeing something like this in person." She pauses for a moment. "Can I take some pictures in here too?"

I nod, and she wanders around, taking pictures of the mushrooms in this chamber. I watch her face light up with each new mushroom she sees.

It is strange with her here, but I go back to tending to my mushrooms. I check all the newest ones first to see if any need extra magic poured into them. Once they are tended to, I check to see if any others are struggling to survive.

As I'm working, I realize that it's quite peaceful with Lydia here. I like hearing the little noises she makes. She gasps frequently about things that she has discovered. She also talks to herself as she explores. It's the opposite of the silence I usually live in.

Eventually, Lydia comes back near me. "Hey, Wold, do you happen to have anything to eat? I'm getting pretty hungry. I have some snacks in my bag, but unfortunately nothing that really counts as a meal. Water would be nice too. My bottle is empty." With that she turns her...bottle...upside down and a couple of drops of water hit the ground.

I gesture toward the pond at the back of the cave. "You can refill your *bottle* with water from there."

She glances at me uncertainly, then looks at the pond. "Is that water safe to drink? I don't think I can just drink untreated pond water."

Ah, right. I remember now that I have heard that humans are sensitive to things. It is very easy for them to get sick from eating or drinking the wrong thing.

I nod. "Yes, you will be safe drinking this water. It is of the Fae Realm, so it is clean."

She gives me a skeptical look, but then says, "Okay."

Then I add, "If you want food, I will have to hunt something for us to eat. Do you like hoppers?"

She looks at me confused. "Hoppers?"

"Yes, they are small fuzzy animals that hop quickly everywhere. They have long ears and like to eat plants. They have tons of babies."

Her eyes get big. "You mean rabbits? You eat rabbits?"

I nod.

Her eyes are still huge when she says, "But they are so cute. I don't know if I could eat one. What about not cute animals? Like rats. Can you hunt those?"

I recognize the word *rat;* they are the small scuttling vermin with bare tails. I stare at her for a moment, then I say, "You would rather eat a rat than a hop—erm, a *rabbit*?"

She starts laughing. "Okay, that does sound pretty ridiculous when you put it like that. No, I don't really want to eat a rat. I guess rabbit will be fine. Do I have to see their cute little faces though?"

I stare at her for a couple of moments. How do humans survive in the world?

"No, I can clean it before you see it." It has been a long time since I have cleaned a kill, so it's probably best if she doesn't see me do it. "I will hunt for hoppers. It is getting dark; you stay in the cave where it is safe."

She smiles. "Okay, thank you, Wold."

***

In no time, I chase down two hoppers and kill them. I skin and clean them, then begin preparing the pelts for drying. It has been years since I have taken the time to do any of this.

I have only just met this Lydia, yet I am taking all this time to prepare food for her. And I am preparing pelts to dry so that she may have something nice to snuggle with.

I don't understand the hold that she has on me.

I take the pelts to a nearby cave so they will dry properly.

I then realize that she will probably want her hopper cooked, so I gather wood and kindling to make a fire and a spit.

All this work just to feed one little human female.

Chapter 6

AFTER WOLD LEAVES, I walk around the cave and explore a little more. I don't recognize any of these mushrooms either, so I guess they must only grow in the fae world.

I still can't believe I'm seeing all of this. I can't believe all of this is happening. I get picked up by a *fae forest guardian monster* that has mushroom growing magic. He may love mushrooms even more than me. I mean, what are the odds?

Also, if I'm being really honest...he's kind of hot. At first, I was afraid of him because of the blood and the claws and well...all of it. But now that I'm around him, I can tell that he's actually trying to be sweet. He seems to be going out of his way to make me comfortable around him. And the way he is awkward when I get near him is adorable.

His face is very similar to a human's, except for the green skin...and the pointed ears...and the huge wide-set fangs that hint at an impossibly large mouth. Okay, so maybe not that similar to a human's, but his face is very attractive. If his face were on a human, I would fling myself on him.

Once I adjust to the differences, his body is attractive too. He's muscular in all the right places. He has a cute butt, and the tail makes it even better. Especially since he got so shy about me touching it.

I was sneaking peeks at him while he was working, and...well...I can't figure out where his cock is. Certainly he has one. I wonder what it looks like...

"Oh no, Lydia, are you seriously falling for a monster?!" I shake my head. No of course not. I can't be. He isn't human, and I can't figure out where his cock is. He has to have some sort of cock though, right? Oh my gods, what if it's weird looking?! I shake my head again. I have to find something else to think about.

I study the pool of water, and it looks like it gets deeper in the middle near the waterfall. I wonder if I could swim in it. I dip my hand in the water to see what temperature it is, and it's delightfully cool. It would feel amazing to swim in. I think about it for a minute and decide that Wold will probably be gone for a little while hunting. I can take a quick dip, and he will never know.

I grab the small towel out of my bag. It's more like a hand towel instead of a full-sized towel, but I can still dry off with it. I slip my clothes off and leave them in a messy pile near the edge of the water. I also take my antler headband off and put it on top of the pile of clothes.

Goose bumps cover my skin as I stand in Wold's mushroom cave completely naked. It gives me a little thrill in my belly like the feeling you get when you are doing something that you know you shouldn't be.

I wade out into the water, and the deepest part only comes up to my ribcage. I relax in the pool for a while, enjoying the feel of the water on my skin. I'm floating on my back with my eyes closed, thinking about Wold and wondering if he knows how to kiss, when I hear a noise. I open my eyes and see Wold standing at the edge of the pool staring at me. I immediately crouch and submerge myself up to my neck. "Oh my gods, Wold, you startled me! I'm so sorry. I just wanted to go for a quick swim, and I thought you would be gone longer."

He doesn't respond. I watch him and he's just staring at me, and I can see that all of his muscles are tense. I could swear that his eyes are glowing brighter as he looks at me. He takes two steps forward and his feet are now in the water, but he stops without going deeper.

He's still not saying anything, so I say, "Wold, are you okay?"

He takes two more steps into the water. His stare is so intense that it's honestly making me a little nervous. I say his name again, but he doesn't seem to respond. His brightly glowing eyes are tracking me. Suddenly, he shakes his head like he's throwing something off, and he seems to recover and act more like himself.

I hesitantly repeat, "Wold, are you okay?"

He growls a little, and I swear I can see his nostrils flare from here. Then he says, "Lydia, what are you doing?"

"I just wanted to go for a swim. Did I do something wrong?"

He sighs, "No, but you aren't careful. You need to be more careful. You don't know the danger that you put yourself in. You are like a little mischievous sprite, flitting around things that could hurt you."

There is something about his voice that makes me shiver a little. "Danger from what?"

The noise he makes is halfway between a growl and a groan. "Danger from me. I am a monster, Lydia. You should be afraid of me."

I shake my head. "No, you're not. Whatever it is that you are worried that you will do, you won't. You won't hurt me." I realize then that I truly believe this. If he was going to hurt me, he would have by now. Instead, he has been kind to me and is caring for me.

"You don't know that. I—"

"Whatever you are about to say, it's not true. You aren't going to hurt me. I trust you."

He groans again and says, "You can't trust me. You don't know me."

I shake my head again. "No. I trust you. There is something about you that draws me to you. I trust whatever force is pushing us together, so I trust you. You aren't meant to hurt me."

Now I notice his big hand is holding something near his groin. I can see a glow from behind his hand and I wonder if it's bioluminescent mushrooms, but why would he hold a bunch of mushrooms there? I look at him more closely and I take in his demeanor. I suddenly realize he's not holding glowing mushrooms. He's holding his *glowing* cock.

My stomach flips. I stand up, which completely bares my breasts to him. Then I begin walking toward him. I can see him visibly tense as I walk closer to him. As the water gets shallower, more and more of my body is exposed. By the time I am right in front of him, I'm completely naked.

I start to feel excitement and heat pooling in my belly.

All of his muscles are tense; it's as if he's holding himself back from something.

I place my hand on his chest, and I notice how warm his skin feels. I look into his glowing eyes and say, "Wold, you aren't going to hurt me. Trust yourself. Trust whatever this is that's bringing us together."

He groans and closes his eyes.

He doesn't seem to mind my touch, so I begin sliding my hand down his chest and onto his stomach. I can see his breathing hitch when I do this. His eyes are locked onto me, and I quietly say, "Wold, you won't hurt me. Trust yourself."

He drops his hand from his cock, and now I can see what he was hiding. It's bioluminescent, so it glows just like the mushrooms in his cave. He's already hard and it's huge, which makes sense because he's huge. It's much larger than any cock I've ever seen. There are ridges that run along the shaft, and they look like they'd feel amazing. There's also something that seems to be wrapped around the base of it, kind of like a cock ring, except I can tell it's a part of him. Suddenly whatever it is starts uncoiling and moves on its own, and I gasp. It's like a vine, but it's bumpy almost like a thick string of beads. It unwraps from around his cock, coiling in on itself a couple of times. Then it uncoils and wraps back around the base of his cock.

I look up at Wold with wide eyes. He's just watching me study him. His glowing eyes lock with mine. He reaches his hand out and runs the knuckles of his fingers along my jaw, then lightly presses the claw of his thumb against my bottom lip. I whimper a little at his touch.

He locks eyes with mine again, and says, "Do you trust me, my little sprite?"

"Yes," I whisper.

He growls and says, "You shouldn't."

I start to say, "Don't s—"

His growl cuts me off. Then he says, "Run."

I stare at him, startled. "What?"

He gives me a wide devilish grin, showing off his huge fangs. "Run."

Chapter 7

I GASP, THEN I run.

I run straight out of the cave and keep going. I hop over any twigs or roots that I see poking up.

The sun is setting, and it's already getting dark in the forest, so it's pretty hard to see where I'm going. I don't even know where to go.

I get a short distance away, and I hear an echoing roar coming from Wold's cave. I scream and run faster, not caring about the sting of sticks when I step on them.

My mind is racing. Is he playing with me, or is he really hunting me? This has to be a game; he seemed so sweet before...

I hear something that sounds like tearing wood, and I look over my shoulder. I can see Wold's shadowy shape and glowing eyes halfway up a huge tree trunk. He seems to be hanging on with his claws and tail. He leaps to the next trunk and grabs on with his claws, tearing small chunks out of the trunk as he does. He keeps chasing me this way, leaping from tree to tree.

Oh gods, he *is* a monster. Real fear begins to bloom inside me. What was I thinking trusting him? What is wrong with me? I even took my clothes off to swim!?

As I look over my shoulder again, he lets out a loud growl, and then a roar. I cover my mouth, holding in a scream, and keep running. Fear and a tiny bit of excitement coil in my stomach and create a terrifying longing that goes straight to my groin as I run.

I look over my shoulder again to see where he is, and my shin slams into an exposed root. I cry out as I fall, sprawling face down on the ground.

Suddenly Wold drops down in front of me. I look up to see him stalking towards me. He lets out a feral growl.

I scream and scramble to my feet again. I turn to run when he suddenly tackles me. He twists us to soften the blow, but he still ends up on top of me.

I'm trembling beneath him, face down in the dirt. I feel his big body press against mine for just a moment, and I feel his cock against my butt. I whimper. Then he flips me over and cages me with his huge body. I'm panting and shaking as I look at him, and I see the ferocious gleam in his eye.

The vines intermixed with his hair grow and reach toward me. I gasp as they wrap around my wrists. Wold uses his claws to tear through where they connect to his scalp. There is a snarled mass of exposed tree roots near my head at the base of a large tree, and Wold wraps the ends of the vines around one of its roots.

I whimper and shiver when he yanks the vines tight; my hands firmly bound above my head.

Wold wraps his big hand around my jaw and tilts my head to the side. I can feel the bite of his claws. He runs his nose along my throat, and I hear him breathe deeply. It makes me shiver again.

My voice is a small whisper when I ask, "What are you going to do with me?"

He just growls, and it sparks fear and arousal in me.

He slowly runs his face down my neck and onto my chest. He stops between my breasts, his face nuzzled to my breastbone. He takes another deep breath, and licks up the length of my breastbone and up my throat with a long, sinuous, forked tongue. I gasp.

My nipples are aching with longing. He lightly nips at the base of my throat, and I let out a quiet whimper. He growls at that.

He moves his hand from my jaw and runs it down my body straight to my pussy. I cry out as he runs his knuckles through my already slick folds. He drags one knuckle back and begins circling my clit, and I moan loudly.

He leans close to my face and growls, "Tonight, I am going to fuck you in my forest, make you scream my name to the gods, and fill you with my seed, my little sprite. Then all of the Fae Realm will know I have claimed you as mine."

Oh. Another moan escapes me.

He gazes at me and his eyes look completely feral. "Are you afraid, little sprite?"

I take in a shaky breath, then say, "Y-yes."

"Good."

I whimper.

He lifts his knuckles, now shining with my juices, to his mouth and licks them clean with that long tongue. He lets out a long, low groan as he tastes me. His voice is barely more than a growl as he says, "I can't wait any longer to feast on you."

I gasp. "Wold...what do you mean?" My voice sounds squeakier than it usually does.

He sits up and lifts both of my feet and places them so my knees are bent, and my ankles are near my thighs. His hair vines grow and wrap around my thighs and ankles, binding them to each other. When both bindings are tight,

Wold uses his claws to tear through the ends of the vines. He gives me that devilish grin again. "You will see."

Then he spreads my legs, baring all of me to him, and lets out a groan as he buries his face between my thighs. I cry out as he slowly licks my pussy and then circles my clit with that impossible tongue. Relief and pleasure explode through me.

"Oh fuck, Wold!"

He growls in response, which sends vibrations through his tongue and straight into my clit, and I gasp at the sensation.

He continues to slowly lick me, then he circles his tongue around my core and thrusts it into me. It feels amazing. How is his tongue so long and thick? He continues to thrust it into me, and gods, it feels so good. He's hitting my g-spot perfectly, rubbing his tongue along it. I moan and writhe against his mouth. He's filling me with his tongue, and I realize that his mouth feels huge. It feels like his mouth is covering me from my butt to almost my pubic bone. How is he doing that? I look down and realize that his mouth is bigger than it normally is. It's like he can unhinge it wider than a regular mouth, and I see a lot more teeth.

His jaw is open wide, and I can feel his fangs press against my skin, then he thrusts his tongue into me again, completely filling me. I decide that I no longer care how he's doing it, because it feels *amazing*. He continues fucking me with his tongue until I'm a moaning, gasping mess, pulling against the bindings. I'm on the edge of an orgasm; I just need a little more to get there. Breathlessly, I start begging him. "Wold...I need more."

He chuckles deeply and doesn't comply. Somehow, he thrusts even more of his tongue into me.

I gasp and beg again. "Please, Wold, let me come."

I feel something rub my clit, and I nearly scream because it feels so good. It must be the forked tip of his tongue. Oh gods, is his tongue long enough to double up inside me and have the forked end come back out? He continues teasing my clit with the tip of his tongue, and my orgasm tears through me. I scream his name as I come, just like he said I would.

He pulls his tongue out of me and continues to gently lick me through the aftershocks of my orgasm.

When he's done, he trails that long tongue up my body and back to my neck, where he leisurely licks my throat. While he licks my throat, he reaches down and uses a claw to cut the vines binding my legs. I stretch them, then wrap my legs around his hips, pulling him close so I feel his cock against me. He groans against my neck, then slides his cock into my pussy.

I gasp as he presses into me. He's huge, and I can feel him stretching me. Then I feel his ridges and—oh gods, they are amazing. I can feel each one as he slowly thrusts into me, filling me so full I feel I might split apart.

Just when I think I can't possibly fit any more, I feel his hips against mine, and he groans as he sinks all the way into me.

I feel the texture of the strange tendril that he has around the base of his cock. As it rubs against me, it sends little sparks of pleasure straight to my core.

His tail comes up to wrap around my waist, tying me to him.

Wold pulls his hips back, and I feel all those glorious ridges coming back out. I look down and realize that I can see the glow of his cock lighting up our stomachs and thighs. When he thrusts back into me, the glow disappears inside me.

He thrusts into me harder and faster. I feel his tendril unwinding and moving, then it loops around on itself so that it's hitting my clit perfectly with each thrust.

"Oh gods, Wold!"

Wold is slamming into me now. He's groaning and growling like a beast, and I can feel another orgasm building. He thrusts into me a few more times, and then I cry out as I come. I can feel my pussy pulse around his cock as my orgasm crashes through me. He thrusts into me one final time, and then he roars as he comes inside me, filling me with his cum.

Chapter 8

My pulse is pounding in my ears as I look at Lydia pinned beneath me. Her skin is flushed the prettiest color. Her eyes are wide as she looks at me, but I don't think she is afraid. She just looks surprised.

When I came back from hunting, the cave had been saturated in her scent. Not just her regular scent either, I caught strands of arousal mixed in with her scent as well. Her scent was so strong and so consuming that I lost myself in it, and the monster in me took over. Now that I have hunted her and claimed her, I can think—and see her—more clearly.

We are both still panting when my cock slides out of her and back into me. She lets out a little "Oh!"

Gods, she is amazing. But what have I done? She's a little human, I didn't even know a human could mate with a fae

Guardian. I didn't really believe that she would be able to take my cock, but she took it, and she seemed to enjoy it. But, gods, I was so careless, I could have hurt her.

We both stare at each other for a few moments.

I finally say, "Lydia...did I...hurt you?"

She shakes her head.

With a sigh of relief, I lower my face to her throat again and breathe in her scent. Then I cut the binding around her hands with my claws and help her lower her arms. She sighs again as I rub up and down each arm.

She cautiously smiles at me. "Thank you. I didn't realize how stiff they had gotten."

I stand up and help her to her feet. She gasps after she stands up. She's looking down, and I see that my seed is running down her thighs.

She gives me a wide-eyed look. "Your cum is bioluminescent?!"

Her word "cum" confuses me, so I say, "Cum? Do you mean my seed?"

She nods her head quickly. "Yes, seed. But seriously, it glows?!"

I rub the back of my neck, a little embarrassed. "Yes, but it won't glow for very long. It will stop soon."

She continues to look down. "Wow."

It's dark now, and we should go back to the cave. I consider all the sticks and rocks beneath my paws, and I look at her bare feet. Gods, I chased her out here without anything to protect her feet. Her feet are so soft and so small. I can only imagine how painful it was for her to run from me.

"Would you like me to carry you back to the cave? So you don't hurt your feet."

She takes a step forward and grimaces when she steps on a stick. "Yes, that would be nice."

I pick her up and carry her back to the cave. I set her down near her stack of clothes by the pond, and I look around helplessly. I don't have anything to help her clean up with.

She must see the concern on my face, and she says, "Don't worry, I have a towel that I can use. I used to run around some woods at my family's vacation home, and one time I fell into a creek when we were there in the winter. It was a shallow creek, but because of the way I slipped, I slid in, so I was soaked from my ribcage down to my feet. I learned then that it was good to have something with me to dry off with. That was a very cold day for me."

As she's talking to me, she's nonchalantly wiping up my seed, and she pauses what she's doing to give me a big smile. Then she continues, "From then on, I've always taken at least a small towel with me when I go out exploring. You never know when you might end up falling in water...or having to clean up bioluminescent seed that's running down your thighs." She gives me a wink when she says that.

I'm still just staring at her. She's being so casual. Are all humans this casual about mating?

While I'm studying her, I notice the hoppers from earlier laying on the ground of the cave. I pick them up and show them to Lydia. "Are you still hungry?"

Her face lights up and she says, "Yes, food would be great!"

I pause for a minute, and then say, "Do you need it cooked?"

She pauses what she's doing and gives me a very strange look. "Yes...do you eat them raw? Wait, don't answer that. I don't think I want to know." She takes a deep breath, then she continues, "Yes, I would like mine cooked, please."

"I will build a fire in front of the cave, and we can cook them there." I tell her as I gather up some things I will need for cooking.

I remember that humans like their meat seasoned, and I frown at the realization that I do not have anything to season the meat with. I tell her this. By this point, she is pulling on her clothes, and she pauses and says, "That's okay. Don't worry about it." She looks at me thoughtfully. "Can we eat any of the mushrooms in here?"

"Some of them." I walk toward a wall and pick a couple of larger ones. "These are very popular to eat among the Elven."

She looks at them as she finishes pulling on her clothes, and says, "Those are huge! We have portobello mush-rooms in my world, but these are bigger. Are they only here in your world? Is it safe for me to eat them?"

I nod a response to both of her questions, and then tell her I will cook them with the hoppers.

As I'm about to go outside to build the fire, Lydia says, "Um, Wold?" I turn to look at her. "Is there somewhere I can use the restroom?"

I cock my head, "Restroom? Do you need to rest?"

She gets a shy smile and blushes a little, then says, "No, I need to pee...to um...relieve myself."

Ah, I see. I show her a place outside a little distance away from the cave where she can relieve herself. I stand by her to watch over her and keep her safe.

She gives me another shy smile and says, "Um, can I have a minute of privacy?"

This is curious to me. She is shy about relieving herself? She was not shy when she was naked and swimming, and she certainly wasn't shy when we were mating. Why would she be shy now? "We mated, why are you shy about this?"

She laughs nervously and says, "I don't know, people are just shy about it. Most people see it as something gross."

"But it is normal, and something everyone does. Why would it be gross?" I ask. She shrugs her shoulders and gives me a nervous look. Okay, if she is shy, then that is fine. "I will be just over here waiting for you."

She sighs with relief and says, "Thank you" before stepping behind a large bush.

I walk a little distance away. I can still see her and scent her, but I suspect she doesn't realize that.

Humans are strange creatures. I try to think of what I know about them. Until now, I've never been around them except for when they must be dealt with because they enter my territory. I have heard of the Elven taking humans as mates, or more likely stealing them and forcing them to be mates. But I do not know what comes of that. I do not know if children come from those matings. I try to remember back to when I was a child and lived at my birth mother's. But humans were never to her taste.

Lydia interrupts my thoughts when she reappears from behind the bush. We walk back to the cave together and I take my cooking supplies outside.

There is a log from a felled tree that I moved near the cave ages ago. It's a good place for us to sit while the food cooks, so I build the fire near it. Lydia perches on the log and watches me put the hoppers on a spit. Then I cook the mushrooms on a hot stone for her. When they are done cooking, I end up using my claws to hold the mushrooms for Lydia while she leans in to take a bite; they are too hot for her to hold.

She laughs and says, "I take it that you don't get many guests."

"No."

She takes the mushroom from me once it's cooled off enough for her. "This is really good, Wold. Thank you."

We sit beside each other in companionable silence for a few minutes while the hoppers cook. Lydia breaks the silence. "Why are you all alone here? If you don't mind me asking."

"I am a Guardian, and this is my territory to protect, so I live here and protect it."

"But what does that mean? What is a Guardian?"

I try to explain. "There are two main types of fae people, The Elven and the Guardians. The stories that humans tell of the fae are usually Elven. They are exceptionally beautiful, with very human-like features. They have pointed ears like these." I gesture to my own ears. "There are also

Guardians. Guardians are protectors of nature and magic. Humans that run across us usually call us monsters, because we are monstrous." I gesture to my body.

Lydia grabs my hand and says, "Wold, you aren't monstrous. You shouldn't say that about yourself." I give her a long look. "Okay fine, you are scary when you lurk in the shadows and all someone can see is your glowing eyes. But you aren't a monster." Then she clasps our hands together.

I smile at that, then I continue. "We have territories that we protect throughout the realm. We inherit them from our fathers."

She says, "So this was your father's territory? Did he die, is that how it passed to you?"

I rub the back of my neck. "Not exactly. This is the territory that my birth mother said was my father's. She brought me here when I was old enough to care for it. At the time, my father was still alive. I do not know if he is anymore."

She furrows her brow, and says, "You don't know who your father is?"

I shake my head. "Not really. My birth mother is Elven. You see, over time many of the Elven have become corrupt and depraved. Some of them like to take Guardians...as their captive lovers. Usually the Guardian is captured and taken to the Elven's estate. They live there in confinement and are forced to please the Elven that has captured them. My birth mother had several Guardians trapped at her estate. My father was one of them, but I've never met him."

I take a deep breath and glance at Lydia to see how she is reacting to this, and she has a horrified look on her face.

I push on. "When my birth mother got pregnant, she had also taken a lot of Elven lovers. She hoped that I would be Elven like them. If she had known that I would be a Guardian, she would have destroyed me while I was still in her womb. When I was born...as soon as she saw me, she knew I was from one of the Guardians. I assume she knew which was my father because I bore his resemblance."

"Oh my gods, Wold, that is horrible. I'm so sorry that your birth mother was like that."

I nod an acknowledgement. "After I was born, my birth mother couldn't risk killing a baby without repercussions, so she brought in a female Guardian as a nursemaid for me. That female fed me and changed me and raised me until I was 7 years old. She was more of a mother to me than my birth mother. My birth mother couldn't wait to get rid of me though, so as soon as she thought I might be able to survive on my father's territory, she brought me here and left me. My nursemaid fortunately convinced my birth mother to let her stay with me for a month to show me what I needed to do to survive here. She's the one that taught me everything I know. She helped me perform the magic to bind myself to my territory. She taught me to hunt, and how to build a shelter. She also taught me how to care for my territory with my magic. When the month was up, she had to go back to my birth mother's home. Then I was alone."

Lydia squeezes my hand, and I suddenly realize that she's still holding it from earlier. "Oh Wold, your birth mother sounds awful. I'm sorry you had to go through that."

I study our hands clasped together, with my 3 fingers fitting perfectly between her 4. And for the first time, I notice how close she's sitting to me. She's talking about her family, but I'm not listening. I'm so focused on her body's proximity to mine. I want to keep her, I need to keep her, but I know I can't. I can't provide the life she needs. I'm a Guardian. I live in the woods like an animal. Gods, if one of the Elven found her...

I interrupt her. "Lydia, we need to find a way to get you home."

Her face falls a little with that, and she lets go of my hand.

I quickly continue. "It's not safe for you here. A lot of the fae are like my birth mother, and if one of them got ahold of you, they wouldn't let you go."

After a moment, she nods. "Okay, then how do we do it?"

"You came through to my world because you accidentally found a thin spot," I explain. "We can look for other thin spots, but those are unpredictable, and no one can tell when or where one will pop up. We could look every day for months and we still may not find one. There is magic that can get you through the barrier, but we will need to buy a few supplies to do that kind of magic. There is a travelling fae market that stops just outside of my territory every new moon, when the night is it's darkest. They will have the supplies we need."

"When is the next new moon?" Lydia asks.

"In three days."

Chapter 9

THREE DAYS.

That's all I will have with Wold.

I'm a little sad that he wants me to leave so soon. Maybe it's crazy, but I was hoping after the wild sex that he would want me to stay. I'm not ready to go home yet. There's a whole world here that I knew nothing about. I want to learn more about it and explore it.

If I'm honest, I also want to learn more about Wold and get to know him. I like him. It's not really like me to get attached to someone so easily, but something just feels right about him to me, and I don't want to leave him.

I need to shake the sadness off though. Moping around isn't going to get him to want me to stay.

I guess I'll just have to show him what he could have if I stayed.

Wold interrupts my thoughts. "The hoppers are done, but we need to let them cool."

Absently I say, "Okay."

I watch him as he moves the spit out of the fire and toward where I am sitting. I'm thinking about what happened earlier in the woods, when he chased me down and fucked the hell out of me. I want him to fuck the hell out of me again, but I'll probably need to convince him to since he seems so worried about hurting me.

I guess I might as well get started showing him what he could have. I mean, there's no time like the present. Except my stomach chooses this moment to growl. Okay, maybe *that* can wait until after I eat.

Wold looks over at me because he heard my stomach too. "You can start pulling pieces off if you want."

That's exactly what I do. The moment the first piece hits my tongue, I realize just how hungry I am. I feel like a wild animal devouring the rabbit as I tear chunks off of it as quickly as I can. It's been a long time since I've eaten and I'm famished. I usually don't eat breakfast, and I forgot to eat lunch because I was too excited about foraging for mushrooms.

Wold eats his so quickly that I'm honestly not sure if he chewed it. I also think he ate it bones and all, but I'm choosing to ignore that.

When I'm done, I lick my fingers and say, "Is it okay if I go inside and rinse my hands off in that pool of water?"

He nods and I go into the cave. I rinse my hands and mouth off with water, then I dry them off with the towel I brought. Then I remember that I used that same towel to wipe Wold's cum off my thighs. Maybe it's time to wash the towel too.

I dunk the towel in the water and try to rinse it as best I can, all while thinking about how good it felt when his mouth was on me, and how amazing those ridges on his cock felt. I was afraid when he chased me, but I was also incredibly aroused.

Wold walks in then. "Are you okay, Lydia?"

I was so lost in thought that I jump when I hear his voice. I reply with, "Yep. Just rinsing out this towel. It's getting kind of dirty." I wring it out and then spread it out on a rock in hopes that it will dry some. When I turn around, Wold has gone very still and is staring at me. I can see some of that feral gleam in his eye. I look at him for a minute, wondering what he's doing. Then I remember that this is how he reacted before he chased me earlier. I'm turned on just from thinking about what we were doing earlier, I wonder if he can smell it. "Wold, are *you* okay?"

He doesn't answer.

"Wold..." I start.

With a rasp, he says, "Lydia..."

I walk up to him and take his hand and lead him into the bioluminescent room that I woke up in when he first found me. "Come with me, Wold."

This seems to rouse him from his trance a little bit, although I don't want him shaken out of it too much. I have plans for him in here.

None of the mushrooms are glowing, so the room is dark. I look at Wold. "Can you do what you did to make them glow?"

Without saying anything, he presses his hand to the wall, and they all begin to glow. It's so beautiful. I've truly never seen anything like it in all my life.

I lead him to the large table like rock in the middle of this chamber, and I sit down. Wold is still standing and staring at me, so I pat the spot next to me and say, "Come, sit with me." He sits, but continues to watch me.

He seems to relax a tiny bit over the next couple of minutes. Well, I don't know if he actually relaxes, but he quit staring at me.

"Hey, Wold?"

He looks at me now, watching and waiting for whatever question I have.

"Do your people kiss?"

He gives me a slightly confused look and says, "I don't know what that is."

"I can show you." I notice that his tail is nervously slapping the ground behind us. "Lean toward me."

He does, and I kiss him. He briefly startles, tensing. But he quickly softens against my mouth and kisses me back. His kiss is a little clumsy at first, but he quickly gets the hang of it. I run my tongue along the seam of his lips to get him to open for me. When he does, I tease his tongue with mine, and he groans low in his throat. His tongue is smooth and silky. I can feel the split tip of it. It feels so much different than mine. He deepens our kiss, and I can feel the press of his fangs against my lips.

I slide my leg across his lap and straddle him. He groans again and cups my ass with those giant hands. I break our kiss and begin trailing kisses along his jaw and onto his neck.

In a husky voice he says, "Lydia…" I continue kissing his neck ignoring him. "Lydia…I can't control…it's not safe."

Between kisses I say, "Safe for whom?" Then I use my teeth to nip his ear.

He groans and his whole body shudders. "Safe for you."

I'm still kissing his neck when I say, "It's safe. You won't hurt me. You didn't hurt me last time." Then I pull my shirt over my head and take my bra off immediately after. Wold groans and palms my breasts in his hands.

I can feel the hard ridge of his cock, and I can see its glow coming from under me. I bite my lip and grind myself against it.

With a groan, he begins running his nose down my throat toward my chest. He inhales, and he sighs. "I'm afraid of hurting you."

I look at his glowing eyes, and say, "You won't. But, I have an idea."

He tilts his head curiously.

"Lay back."

He just stares at me like I've lost my mind.

Again, I say, "Lay back on the boulder." He does, and I grab each of his hands and put them straight up over his head.

"Those vines you used to tie me, can you make some?" The vines in his hair start growing longer. I begin wrapping them around his wrists and I use my teeth to cut them once his hands are bound together. I spit out the bitter green taste of them, then I use the rest of the length to tie his hands to a large, exposed root near his head. Then I look at him and say, "There. you don't need to worry about hurting me."

He watches me and I can swear that his eyes are glowing brighter now, and I hear his tail swat the boulder.

I stand up with one foot on either side of his stomach, then I pull my pants and underwear off. I lower myself back down to straddle his stomach. Then I lean down and kiss him.

When I move to kiss his neck again, he says in a whisper that sounds like a growl, "Lydia, I need to taste you." I bite my lip and smile. He wants me to sit on his face.

I slide up his body and work my knees into place on each side of his face between his arms and head.

Before I can even lower myself onto him, I feel that long tongue lightly brush against my pussy. I gasp, and I hear a low growl in his throat. There's another light brush of his tongue against my pussy, and I start to lower toward his face. I'm craving more of that tongue. The next touch is firm as he slides his tongue through the folds of my pussy and circles my clit with that deliciously forked tip.

It feels so good that it makes my body weak, and I lean forward and grasp his antlers so I can hold myself up. He continues to lick me, each brush of his tongue making me moan. When he thrusts his tongue inside me, I cry out. He expertly rubs my g-spot as he thrusts that amazing tongue into me. With each thrust, his tongue goes deeper inside me until I'm completely filled by it.

I can feel the press of his fangs against me, and I look down to see that his jaw is open wide again. I'm rocking my hips against his face when I feel the tip of his tongue come back out of me and press against my clit. I cry out. "Oh fuck, Wold!"

He teases my clit with it, and in the next moment, I'm screaming as I come. I feel that long tongue slide out of me, and then I start to shift my way down his body toward the glow of his cock.

I kiss him before I slide my hips down to meet his. I feel his tail coil up my leg, holding onto me. His cock is huge and leaking glowing cum. I reach down and circle my hand around as much of his girth as I can, then I gently stroke him. Wold groans and bucks his hips up while also pulling against his bindings. His eyes are brighter than I've ever seen them. I stroke him again and watch him gasp and buck more. He groans. "Lydia..."

While stroking him one more time, I say, "Tell me you want to fuck me."

He moans. "Lydia, I need to fuck you."

I slick his cock through my pussy and hold it against my entrance, then I slowly press down on him. His groan turns into a growl as he slides into me. I feel every ridge on his amazing cock as he stretches me as far as I can handle. I moan his name as I rise back up. Then I cry out as I sink back down on him. He fills me so full. I continue to slowly ride his cock. I moan as Wold groans and growls beneath me. "Fuck, Wold, I love how much you fill me up."

Then I feel his tendril uncoil from around the base of his cock, and I gasp when I feel it press against my ass. It's just a slight nudge at first. But then it presses a little more firmly, and I feel it slip in just a little. It makes everything more intense, and I close my eyes tightly and hear myself whimper. Wold whispers, "Lydia..." When I open my eyes, he's searching my face, looking for something. Permission, maybe?

I nod. "It's good...don't stop...just go slow."

The pressure increases and I try to keep my muscles relaxed. He slowly sinks it into me little by little, pausing to let me adjust to the sensation. I moan as the final bit sinks into me, and my pussy convulses around his cock.

Wold lets out a low groan.

I slowly begin to raise and lower myself on his cock and tendril. I gasp and moan as I adjust to both of them moving inside me. I start to speed up my movements and gods, I didn't know it could feel this good. I grind myself against him needing to feel everything. Needing more.

Wold groans. His eyes are glowing so brightly as he watches me ride him. "Use me Lydia."

I slip my hand down and rub my clit while I rock my hips on him. Wold groans as he thrusts into me and watches me. Gods it feels so good, but I still want more. I want him wild. I want him barely able to control himself. I want him to fuck me like a beast.

I gasp, "Wold, I need more. Fuck me. Claim me."

Wold lets out a feral growl, then uses his claws to rip the vines around his wrists. With his hands free, he immediately grabs me by the hips and raises me up until his cock and tendril almost slip out of me, then he buries himself back inside me. I can feel the pinpricks of his claws as he grasps my hips. I cry out, it feels so good.

He flips us over so I am on my back as he looms over me and pounds into me. He leans down and growls as he licks my neck. I'm gasping and can barely breathe from the pleasure. I'm at the very edge of an orgasm when he growls, "Come for me, my little sprite." That's all I need to push me over the edge. I scream. Wold slams his cock into me and roars as he comes. I can still feel my pussy convulsing around him as he fills me with his cum. We are both panting and gasping by the end of it.

Wold leans his forehead against mine. Then he asks, "Did I hurt you?"

I smile and shake my head no, then I reach up and kiss him. "I loved it, Wold."

He lets out a sigh of relief.

I look at his wrists that still have scraps of vine wrapped around them. "You got out of the vines."

He smiles at that, then gently pulls his cock and tendril out of me and shifts to lay beside me. I curl up against his chest and yawn. I look down at his cock, and I notice that now it seems to be retreating inside of him.

"Wold, can I ask about your cock?"

He gives me a confused look.

"I noticed that you can't see it when you are just walking around. Does it go back inside you?"

He tentatively says, "Yes. Is that not what human cocks do?"

"Nope. They stay outside. Do you mind if look at it?"

He shakes his head.

I slide down beside his hips. As his cock gets softer, it retreats inside a slit that looks kind of like a pocket. I run a finger along the slit and Wold sucks in a breath. I look at him. "Is it sensitive?"

"Not as sensitive as my cock, but still sensitive."

"Can I touch it again?"

Wold's eyes seem to glow a little more brightly, and he nods. This time I press two fingers more firmly along the slit. The seam slips and barely opens just enough for my fingertips to dip in the tiniest bit. Wold gasps and I feel his body shudder. When I pull my fingers away, I notice my fingertips are a little slippery and have a slight shine.

Wold must notice me looking at them because he says, "It's to keep the skin from pulling and to help with mating."

"Oh, so you make your own lube."

He studies me for a moment, then buries his clawed fingers in my hair. He gently tugs and says, "Come."

I slide back up beside him, and he tucks me into his side.

"Lydia, you should sleep. It is nearly morning."

I snuggle into his side, and he curls around me. I fall asleep almost immediately.

Chapter 10

Everything is dark when I wake up, and I can't tell if it's day or night. For the briefest moment, I forget where I am. I can't see anything. My heart starts racing, and I feel the prickle of sweat breaking out. But then I roll over and my hand touches the moss-like fur on Wold's back, and I remember everything. I snuggle up to him and fall back asleep.

I wake up later when he moves to get up. "Is it morning?"

"No, it is afternoon. I usually sleep during the day and wake up in the evening."

"Oh. Are you nocturnal?" I ask as I begin putting on my clothes.

"No, I just like the night better," he explains. "There are less humans that I have to deal with at night."

"Humans? Isn't this a different world? What about the wall of magic that I ran into? Isn't it supposed to keep them out?"

He sighs, "Yes, but there are sometimes thin spots like the one that you came through to get here. There have been more thin spots lately, and more humans slip in during the day than at night."

"Oh. What happens to them if they wander in during the day while you are sleeping?" I ask as I try to run my fingers through my tangled hair.

"Part of the magic of the wall is that it repels humans. If one comes through a thin spot, they are usually extremely unsettled once they are on the fae side. It makes them want to turn around and go back. I do not like being the monster that scares people, so I would rather let them wander off on their own. You wandering so far in was unusual."

I pause trying to untangle a stubborn knot in my hair and look at him. "But what if someone gets stuck here in the fae world like I did? Do you just let them wander off?"

His face turns dark, and he's giving me a look that I can't quite read. "I am bound to protect this land. I would be compelled to kill them."

I gape at him for a minute or two, the knots in my hair completely forgotten. When I feel like I can speak again, I say, "Um, Wold...compelled to kill them?! I'm a human trapped here!"

"I know, but I am not compelled to kill you. I am drawn to you. You are the only human that this has happened with. The others either went back on their own, or...I did as the bond demanded."

A shiver wracks my body, and I cross my arms over my chest. I frown as I study his face. "I feel drawn to you too. That's why I kept going once I crossed the creek. I felt pulled in by something," I admit.

He tilts his head and studies me.

"What does that mean, Wold?"

"I do not know," he says. "The way my birth mother raised me...I do not know much about our world. Only enough to survive."

"Am I the only human in this world?" I ask.

"No. I have heard of others. The Elven are not bound to the land, and they are known to steal humans occasionally for their pleasure. They know of ways to bring them in past the Guardians," he explains. "There are spells that can allow the Elven to go through the wall, and they use them to go into the human world to steal people. But I do not know much more than this. My nursemaid told me to never allow any of the Elven to go through the wall in my territory, so I haven't."

"Is that what you meant when you said that we could get stuff from the fae market to send me home?" I ask.

"Yes," he replies.

"Do you know how to do the spell?"

"Yes, my nursemaid taught me. She wanted me to be able to escape my birth mother if I needed to, even if it meant going into the human world," he says.

"You keep calling her your nursemaid, did she have a name?"

I can see the pain on his face when he says, "Yes, I called her Nanni when my birth mother wasn't around. I wasn't allowed to call her anything other than nursemaid when anyone else could hear us."

"That's so sad, Wold. I'm sorry that you had to grow up like that." I pause, then say, "Well, I guess we have a plan. So what do you usually do during the day, er, I mean night?"

"We need to eat, so I will hunt for some more hoppers. Then I usually spend time in the cave tending to the mushrooms. I also survey my territory to make sure nothing is amiss."

"Oh, I would love to see your territory! Can I come with you for that?" I say excitedly.

He looks at me curiously. "Yes."

"Would it be all right if I went for a swim to rinse off and try to get clean first?"

"That will be fine. I will go hunt for hoppers."

Chapter 11

I HUNT DOWN TWO more hoppers for us.

All I can think about is Lydia while I work. I think about the way that she smiles at me. I think about the noises she made when my cock was buried inside her. And her scent, oh gods, her scent. Those thoughts make my cock stiffen. I can feel it press against the seam of its pouch. It's just waiting to pop out at any moment, so I switch to thinking about something else.

I make a mental list of the items I will need for the spell to send Lydia back home.

Lydia. The way she curled into me to sleep, I've never felt so comfortable. It just feels good being near her. How can I send her home? Now that I have her, I don't know if I can let her go.

When I get back to the cave, Lydia is walking around looking at everything. Her hair is still very wet, so she must have recently finished bathing.

Her face brightens when she sees me return. As I watch her, she picks up the false antlers that she wore in her hair yesterday, and she puts them back on.

Watching her casually slip them on her head makes me think about yesterday when I carried her to the cave while she was unconscious. I was horrified when those little antlers fell off. I was worried that it meant she was badly injured. I carefully carried them back with us while I was also carrying her. When I laid her down in the cave, I spent a long time trying to figure out how to reattach them to her head. Imagine my surprise when I realized the stiff band that they were attached to went around her head. Although it doesn't seem like it would be very comfortable to wear, it makes me smile to see her put them on.

"Hey, Wold!" she says. "Did you get more rabbits?"

"Yes, two hoppers."

I light the fire and set them up on the spit to cook. Then I walk back toward the cave and Lydia follows. I begin checking on the mushrooms and feeding them magic if needed. Lydia watches me with a look of wonder on her face.

She finally asks, "Do you do anything with all of them?"

"Some of them I spread around my territory so that they can thrive. All of them are important to nature, but some of them can be used by the fae for different things. Some are edible, and there are others that you can make teas with. There are also some that are used in spells. I can harvest them and sell them to vendors at the fae market."

"Oh wow! Does each territory have its own thing they can grow or make and sell?"

"I do not know. Probably." I've never really thought that much about what other territories might be doing. I've always just tried to survive on mine. Maybe I have isolated myself too much.

"You mentioned a spell; do you mean the kind of spells that witches do?" she asks.

"I do not know what a witch is."

"It's usually a woman that can make magic by mixing herbs and different things, like bones or snakeskin or teeth, into potions or spells for casting magic," she explains. "I don't know if they can actually do magic. They are more like a fairy tale; you just hear stories about them."

I reply, "That sounds a lot like some of the of magic that the fae can do. Perhaps the witches that your tales are about were actually Elven fae that left the Fae Realm to live in your world. Or maybe they were the child of an Elven and a human. I do not know if they can have children with humans, though."

She looks surprised. "Why would they want to leave this world for the human world? Surely my world looks so dull compared to this one."

"I believe Elven families fight each other for power and wealth. Maybe some of them had to run away from a dangerous family member."

I think of my own birth mother as I say this. I realize that I can't even remember what she looked like anymore. I remember what my nursemaid looked like. I remember how kind she was when I was little. She would hug me if I was sad and told me stories to help me fall asleep. I remember the day my birth mother brought me here to leave me. I was so terrified and I had no idea how to live on my own. I can remember the look on my nursemaid's face as she pleaded with my birth mother to let her stay and teach me how to live here. My birth mother did not want to, but eventually relented. I remember my birth mother saying, "I don't see why anyone would care if it survives. The world can do with one less *monster*." She always called me a monster. I've always wondered if she called my father a monster even though she took him to her bed.

She gave my nursemaid a month to teach me. I'll never forget the relief when she was able to stay. That month was so peaceful. It was the most peace I had ever felt in my short life. I enjoyed climbing trees, and helping the mushrooms grow. I even thought prowling to watch for humans was fun. I didn't understand until much later, when I actually saw a human, how awful it would feel to scare everyone away.

When my nursemaid left, a piece of me broke. I cried and begged her to stay, but she knew she couldn't. My birth mother would have come after her and punished both of us for her disobedience if she stayed with me. So, she left.

I cried for days.

I only stopped long enough to hunt and care for my mushrooms. I wanted to make my nursemaid proud. I wanted to do a good job in case she was ever given permission to come back for a visit.

It was soon after she left that I found the small cave that I live in. I felt safe and protected by the roots of the tree, so I began sleeping there.

Several months after my nursemaid left, I had to scare away my first humans. It was a mother and a child that were hiking and playing in the woods. They wanted to dip their feet into the stream at the border.

I didn't really believe I could scare an adult. Certainly I wasn't so much of a monster that an adult would be afraid of me. I must have been the same age as her human child. But they were terrified. They both screamed, and the mother yelled at me to stay back.

It was another year or so before a human came into my territory and didn't turn back to leave. The bloodlust that overwhelmed me from the bond with the land was terrifying. I couldn't control myself when I killed him.

I understood then that I was the monster that my birth mother said I was.

For so long I had craved company in my lonely existence, but after that night, I hoped no one would ever come to see me again. I didn't want the nursemaid to see what I was. Every day I became angrier, sadder, and lonelier.

"Hey, Wold, you okay?" Lydia interrupts my dark thoughts.

"Yes." We've been quietly walking around the cave checking on each mushroom. "I'm not used to having someone here with me while I do this. My mind wandered."

"Okay. Didn't you say that you will also need to go out and survey your territory? I would love to come exploring with you," she says brightly.

"It will be a lot of walking," I warn.

"I don't mind."

By the time I am done tending to all of the mushrooms, the hoppers are well cooked. We let them cool down and eat in comfortable silence until Lydia finally speaks up.

"I like it here. It's so peaceful." She smiles at me.

I watch her. She does seem to like it here. I like her being here too. I like sharing my space with her.

Once we are done eating, we leave to check on my territory.

Lydia is amazed at everything I show her. She squeals with happiness when she sees some of the spots that I've spread the mushrooms to.

One edge of my territory is a cliff. She thought it was beautiful. She made me promise to bring her back when the sun is setting.

Nothing out of the ordinary happens while we are out, but Lydia is excited about everything. She loves everything here. She loves looking at every little plant or flower.

We end up going to the den that I usually sleep in. I show her the opening in the roots, and she carefully lowers herself in.

"Oh, I like it here! It's very cozy," she says.

I touch the wall, and the bioluminescent mushrooms begin glowing. Over the years, I have brought many mushrooms into this den, so the glow is impressive. She gasps once they all are glowing.

"I found this place when I was young. I started bringing mushrooms here as soon as I could because their glow comforted me when I was afraid or alone," I explain.

When she looks at me, she has tears in her eyes.

"It's beautiful, Wold. I'm glad you were able to find something to comfort you back then," she says.

She closes the distance between us and hugs me. I'm so much larger than her that she barely reaches my chest.

I stroke her hair with the claws of one hand while I pull her against me with the other.

We stand there holding each other.

How am I ever going to let her go?

"Wold, I like it here with you."

I just hold her tighter.

She looks at me and says, "Can I try something?"

I nod and watch her.

"Come over here and sit."

Once I sit down, she straddles my lap and leans in to kiss me. I devour her tiny mouth. She's so small and tastes so sweet.

I feel her running her hand down my chest toward my stomach. It's a ghost of a touch, but it sends a wave of pleasure straight to my cock. My cock is already hard and straining against the seam of its pouch. With a gentle touch, she runs her finger along that seam. I gasp as my cock springs free of its pouch. I watch as she grasps my cock in her tiny hand and strokes it. The pleasure takes my breath away, and I groan. My cock looks so big in her hand. It's so big compared to her. I still can't believe that she can take it.

She kisses my neck as she strokes it again. I groan and watch as a bead of precum rolls down my shaft and stops against her fingers. She slowly moves down my body, until her face is level with my cock. I stare as she uses her tongue to lick the precum off my cock. I dig my claws into the ground and groan as a wave of pleasure rolls through my body.

I gasp. "Lydia…"

She whispers, "Shhh. You won't hurt me. Just enjoy it." Then she licks from the base of my cock to the head of it. She closes her mouth around my cock and sucks as much of it into her mouth as she can fit, wrapping her hand around the rest of it.

I groan and growl as pleasure wracks my body. My claws are dug deep into the ground, and my hips are desperate to buck up into her, but I tighten all my muscles to stop them.

I can't hurt her. I can't. I won't.

She moans as she slowly pulls it back out of her mouth and licks around the tip. Then she's sucking it back into her mouth again. I nearly cry out, it feels so good.

I watch as she begins to bob her head up and down on my cock. I'm gasping and groaning as pleasure rolls through me. My body is trembling from both the pleasure and the effort to stay as still as possible. I feel her hum and moan with my cock buried deep in her throat. My groans have become constant growls, and I know I'm close to coming.

I growl, "Lydia..."

She moans again and sucks harder, and then I'm roaring as I come. Pulse after pulse of my seed spills down her throat.

Once she's swallowed it all, she slides my cock out of her mouth and crawls up my body to curl up at my side. I'm gasping for breath.

I manage to rasp, "Lydia..." Then I groan. "Gods...Lydia..."

She giggles. "I guess you liked that."

I pull her onto my chest and kiss her. Devour her is more accurate. I flip us over, so she is on her back with me on top of her, then I start pulling at her clothes. I hook a claw on the waistband of her pants. "Take these off."

"You don't have to—"

I cut her off when I say, "Take these off or I will tear them off."

She squeaks and begins taking them off. She barely has them pulled down when I snake my tongue between her thighs and lick her pussy. She squeals at that, then wiggles away as she takes her pants off.

As soon as her pants are completely off, I grab her hips and slide her back toward my mouth. She moans as I slide my tongue over her pussy, then I work it inside her. I open my mouth wider and thrust my tongue even further. I love the way she tastes, and I love plunging my tongue as far into her as I can so that I am surrounded and consumed by her flavor.

I snake the tip of my tongue back out of her so I can rub her clit with it, and she cries out when I do. She is moaning loudly and grinding herself against my face.

All I can taste, or smell, is her. I am lost in her.

Her moaning turns louder as she nears her release. I rub my tongue against the inside wall of her pussy and continue stroking the tip of my tongue against her clit. Her breath hitches, then she cries out as she comes. Her pussy pulses and squeezes my tongue during her orgasm. When all of her muscles relax and I can tell she is finished, I snake my tongue out of her. Then I lick my way up to her neck.

The desire to bite her and bind her to me is so strong. I fight it every time we mate. My fangs ache to bury into her.

Lydia moans and wiggles beneath me, pulling me from my thoughts. She says, "Wold, please fuck me."

I groan, then position my cock at the entrance to her core and thrust into her. I growl; she feels so fucking good. She squeezes my cock tighter than I could have ever imagined.

As I thrust into her, my tendril unwinds from around my cock. It snakes to the entrance of her bottom and slowly presses in. She gasps and moans even louder.

"Oh fuck, Wold! Don't stop. I'm going to come again!" She screams as she comes, and I groan and snarl as I come a moment later. We are both left panting. I collapse on top of her, then I roll off of her to lay beside her, tucking her into my side.

We lay there, snuggled up together, just talking for what must have been hours. Lydia tells me about her childhood and her world. She is constantly saying that her world is so boring compared to mine, but her world sounds so foreign and strange to me. I'm sure it would seem amazing if I saw it in person.

Earlier we had picked some berries that grow in my territory, and I harvested some of the edible mushrooms. When we get hungry, we eat some of those.

After that, we mate again. Lydia ties my hands to a root again and straddles my face while I fuck her with my tongue until she screams. Then she rides my cock again. I love watching her when she is on top of me. I like watching the way she moves. I like seeing her in control. Just like that last time, I tear through my restraints as she gets close to coming. I flip her over to her back and pound into her until we are both screaming.

With each mating, I am getting more and more confident that I will not hurt her. Maybe Lydia is right; I am not the monster that I have always thought I was.

We are curled up together relaxing, and I can see through the roots that the sun is starting to come up, and Lydia is getting tired. She keeps dozing off while talking. I tell her that we need to get some sleep and tuck her back into my side.

Right before she drifts off, she says, "I love being here with you, Wold."

Chapter 12

I WAKE BEFORE WOLD does. The mushrooms are still glowing with his magic. I can see light through the roots, but I have no idea what time it is, so I roll over and snuggle up to Wold's back. I'm the extra tiny spoon to his really big spoon.

As I'm snuggling with him, I start looking at the mushrooms in his fur. There's a small patch of them on top of his shoulder near my face. They seem to change frequently. Sometimes he has a lot, but sometimes, he doesn't have any. I've noticed that the times that he doesn't have any are usually really soon after we've had sex. I touch one of the mushrooms, and it falls off his shoulder onto the ground. Startled by it, I gasp. Wold groans and rolls over, then he tucks me back into his chest.

I feel so guilty about the mushroom, so I whisper, "Wold, I accidentally knocked one of the mushrooms off your shoulder. I tried to touch it. I'm sorry, I didn't know that I would hurt it."

He chuckles deep in his throat, then says, "Do not fret, they fall off all the time. It is just what they do."

"So I didn't hurt you? Why do they grow?" I ask.

"No, you did not hurt me." He shrugs his shoulders. "I do not know why they grow. It is just part of my magic, just like the vines in my hair."

We snuggle and doze off and on for a while before we finally get up and begin Wold's tasks. By that time, the sun is setting.

We head back to the mushroom cave, and Wold goes out and hunts us some more rabbits while I take a dip in the little pool. As I get out of the water, I look at my little pile of clothes and cringe just a bit. I really don't want to put those back on. They are getting pretty gross after wearing them for a few days. I need to talk to Wold about getting me some new clothes. Maybe we can get some at that market he was talking about. I dry off and slip them back on anyway. Maybe I can wash them in the pool before we go to sleep.

By the time I'm dressed, Wold is back with the rabbits. He brought three back this time. He cooks them on the spit while tending to his mushrooms. Once we are done eating, we head out to care for his territory again. That's how we spend our day.

When we get back to the cave, I tell Wold that I'm going to wash my clothes. I strip off all of my clothes, and I notice that Wold is staring at me from the other side of the cave. He's so still, not moving a muscle, and it looks like he's barely breathing. Excitement zips through my body. It feels like he is hunting me, and I'm pretty sure I know how this is going to end tonight. I scrub my clothes in the water—the best I can do without soap. Maybe we can get some different soaps at the market too. Certainly they have soap there. Right?

I wring out my clothes and lay them out to dry. By that point, the muscles in my arms are burning from exertion, and I'm sweating a little. I wipe the sweat off my forehead and take a deep breath. I had no idea how hard it was to do laundry the old-fashioned way. Once I'm done, I look up at Wold. He is still standing in the same spot, completely still, all of his muscles tense. I know what that means, and my arousal sparks to life. I stare back at him for a moment or two, then I whisper, "Wold."

He springs into action just like a hunter after his prey. He lunges for me and tackles me to the ground, and I squeal as he does. He pins me to the ground on my back and then growls as he licks from my chest up the side of my neck. He nips my neck with his teeth, and I gasp. Then he spreads my legs and absolutely feasts on my pussy until I'm screaming his name and begging him to fuck me. He slides up my body and presses his cock into me, and I watch as the glow from his cock disappears inside me. Then he fucks me in quick strong thrusts. His tendril coils around on itself so that it is positioned perfectly to hit my clit. We are both moaning loudly when we come.

Afterwards, Wold gently kisses me and asks if he hurt me. I think he's going to ask after every time we have sex. I reassure him that he didn't, but he checks my neck where he nipped me anyway. He let out a sigh of relief when he sees that he didn't break the skin.

He picks me up and carries me into the pool so that we can both wash off. He dunks his head under the water, and when he comes back up, I gasp because I haven't seen him like this. He looks so otherworldly. Water drips from his antlers. His long flowing hair is straight and smooth, with the exception of the vines intermixed in his hair. But they are lying flat right now too. Water beads up and sparkles on his fur.

He's breathtaking.

When we are done washing off, we go back to the bio-luminescent mushroom room to sleep.

I snuggle into his chest and just breathe in his earthy scent. Before I fall asleep, I say, "Wold, do they sell things like clothing and soap at the market?"

"Yes, I think so. Why?"

"Can I get some new clothes and a couple of soaps to wash my body and my clothes with?"

Wold is quiet for a minute or two. I look up at him to see if he had fallen asleep. He hasn't. Instead, he has the saddest look on his face. I haven't seen Wold look this sad before. He sighs. "Lydia, you will not need them after tomorrow. We will get the supplies to send you home."

"Wold, I don't want to leave. Can't I stay here with you?" I ask.

He stares at me without answering. I can see the pain in his eyes.

"Please, Wold. I want to stay here with you. I want to be here." I beg, and I can tell I'm on the verge of tears. Tomorrow is the last day. We will go to the fae market and get the things he needs to send me home. I've tried to push it out of my mind and pretend like it wasn't coming, but now it's almost here. Tomorrow. Tomorrow, he will send me away.

He sighs. "Lydia...it's too dangerous in my world. The Elven—"

"No...please, Wold. I've been safe with you here. I will be safe here. This is what I want. I want to be with you." Hot tears are running down my cheeks now. "I don't want to go back. Please Wold, let me stay."

He uses the back of his knuckles to wipe my tears away. "Lydia...I don't want you to go, but I can't keep you safe. Not even Guardians are safe from the Elven. How will I keep you safe when I can't even keep myself safe?"

He curls me into his chest and holds me while I quietly cry myself to sleep.

Chapter 13

My heart breaks at Lydia's tears.

I want to keep her. I want her bound to me as my mate. I want to spend my days with her like we have spent the past few days.

No matter how much I want to, I cannot keep her. It's just not safe. What if she stayed and one of the Elven took her? I could not live knowing she was trapped like that, bending to the whim of some arrogant Elven master.

My father and the other male Guardians that my birth mother imprisoned could not even keep themselves safe. Once one of the Elven decides they want something, they will stop at nothing to get it. If they knew a human was here with me...I would not be able to keep them away.

I ache at this thought. I want her to stay with me with every piece of my soul. I know deep down inside that she was meant for me.

I hold her as she falls asleep. Tomorrow we will harvest mushrooms to sell, then we will buy the ingredients for the spell. Tomorrow, we will send her home.

***

The next morning, I wake earlier than normal because I know I have much work to do. I am in a terrible mood. I do not look forward to anything today. The sun is still up, but the whole world just seems dark. It feels like those first days after my nursemaid left me; those first years alone.

I wake Lydia beside me. She seems to be much more subdued today too. She has none of that happiness that normally radiates from her.

I tell her the plan for today. It is mid-afternoon so we will have extra time, but we still have a lot to do before the market tonight.

I hunt for us and check on my mushrooms as the *rabbits* cook. Lydia accompanies me just the way she has on the other days, but I can see that instead of excitement, she has only sadness. She does not gasp in surprise and wonder at mushrooms. Today, she sniffles and wipes her eyes. I stop and hold her several times throughout my work.

Once I am done caring for the mushrooms and we eat our food, I weave a bag out of my vines. I leave the vines attached to my head so I can make it bigger if I need. Then I begin harvesting the mushrooms that I can sell. I take a lot of them. I don't really know how much the ingredients are going to cost.

If I thought Lydia was sad before, harvesting my precious mushrooms has made it even worse. She helps hold the bag for me, but sniffles and whimpers the whole time.

It is getting dark as I finish harvesting all of the mushrooms I will need. By this point my bag is huge, and has turned into more of a sack. I cut the ends of the vines with my claws and tie off the sack.

I look at Lydia's sad face, then I hug her to me. She presses her face to my chest, and I can hear her muffled crying. I pet her hair. "Shhh, my little sprite. You will see. It will be okay."

She sniffs and wipes her tears. "Wold, it won't be okay. I want to be with you. How will it be okay if I am not with you?"

"Because you will be safe." I tell her, and I hear her sigh.

"It doesn't matter if I am safe if I am broken. Wold, it's going to break me to leave you. I'm meant to be here with you, and I think you know that. The wall let me through so that I could be with you. How else do you explain this force that draws us to each other? The spell that binds you to this land also let me live. It didn't make you kill me. I am supposed to be here with you. Please don't send me away. You feel like home to me." Tears are running down her cheeks again.

Seeing her pain nearly breaks me. What she says makes sense, but none of that matters if the Elven gets her. I have to keep her safe, even if it means sending her back to the human world. I remember the Guardians that my birth mother kept captive. They were big; bigger than me. They were strong, and they were powerful. But none of that helped them. None of that kept them safe in the end. My magic and strength will not be enough to keep her safe.

There is nothing I can say to ease her pain. I feel the same pain. So I just hold her instead. We stand there for a few minutes holding each other, then I say, "We should get ready to leave for the fae market." She looks heartbroken, so I continue. "I think you will love the market. There are going to be so many things for you to see."

She gives me a small, sad smile. "Have you been many times?"

"When I was younger. Not in recent years, though. I gave up most comforts a long time ago," I reply. "I enjoyed going to them when I was young though. It was the only time I got to see others. It allowed me to feel normal for a day."

Before we leave, I take Lydia to a back corner of the cave. There are bunches of small mushrooms that glow faintly. I pick a handful of them. I eat one and then give her another. She looks at me curiously as she chews it up.

"It doesn't taste like much. Is this mushroom for eating?"

"No, this mushroom will protect you from anyone that tries to cast a glamour on you. Some of the Elven are able to do that, and that is how they kidnap people." I explain as I hand the rest to her, "You just eat one a day, and it will break any glamour spells that anyone tries to use on you. If something happens and you need this, you will need to take one at about the same time every day to keep yourself protected."

"Oh...okay. I will. Is it really that dangerous there?" she asks as she digs in her bag. She pulls out a tiny bag and drops the mushrooms into it. Then she tucks the tiny bag into the piece of clothing that she calls a *bra*.

"Yes, it can be. Anytime I need to leave my territory, I always take some with me, just in case." I say. We leave the cave and begin walking toward the inside edge of my territory. "It will take us a while to walk there."

She just nods. She seems distracted and lost in thought. I'm sure I know what is consuming her mind, because it's consuming my mind too.

I don't want her to leave.

Chapter 14

HE WASN'T JOKING WHEN he said it would take us a while to get there. We walk for what feels like a couple of hours. I don't have a watch, and my phone battery and portable charger finally died this morning. So I don't know exactly how long it has been, but it feels like hours.

We walk mostly in silence. I think neither one of us knows what to say. I don't want to leave, and he doesn't want me to either. But I must leave to stay safe.

I thought he was exaggerating about how dangerous it is in his world, until he gave me enough anti-glamour mushrooms for 10 days. Maybe Wold is right; maybe it really is this dangerous.

But I don't understand. I really feel like we are supposed to be together. Why would everything have lined up for us to be together if we were just going to be torn apart in the end?

I cry off and on while we are walking. I try to hide it from Wold, but sometimes he sees me, and he holds me at those times. My thoughts are nothing but sadness and despair.

Wold speaks, and it startles me. "Just ahead is the edge of my territory."

I look where he is pointing, but don't see anything but more woods. "Where? I can't see it."

"No, it's nothing you can see. I can just feel it."

We walk up to a large tree with a gnarled trunk, and he says, "Beyond this tree is no longer my territory."

"Whose territory is it?" I gasp. "Wait. Are they going to try to kill us for being on it?"

"No, that magic is only for the territories on the border of the human world," he explains. "The land beyond my territory is neutral, so anyone can travel on it."

We walk past the tree, and I don't feel any different. I look at Wold. He has a strange look on his face, but I can't really tell what he is feeling. He must be feeling something. "Are you okay? You have a weird look on your face."

"Yes, it feels strange leaving my territory. And I have not done it in a long time, so I am not used to this feeling." He looks a little strained as he says it. "It will be fine though."

"Okay." I'm not convinced though, so I decide to keep an eye on him.

We walk for a little while longer, still in silence. I'm starting to fall back into my sadness, when I hear something that sounds like faint music. I look around, and say, "Wold, is that music? Where is it coming from?"

He smiles and points ahead of us. "It's from the market. It's not that far away now. Pretty soon you will be able to see the lights from it."

This perks me up a bit. I'm still devastated about leaving Wold, but I am excited to see the market. I don't even know what to imagine it looks like. And now I know there is music!

After we walk a little bit further, I am able to see the glow of lights. And it's so beautiful.

"How do they have lights? Do they have electricity like in the human world?"

"No, they are magic lights," he replies. "There are many types of spells for lights."

I gasp. "Really?! Why do you not have any?"

He shrugs. "I used to get them, but after a while it didn't seem to matter. I can see in the dark, and I like my mushrooms better."

I smile and slip my hand into his. "I like your mushrooms too. They are the most beautiful thing I've ever seen."

We walk toward the market, hand in hand.

I can see more details as we get closer. It looks like an old-fashioned carnival! There are floating lights everywhere. They look like little orbs that just hang in the middle of the air. Some of them are bright, some of them are soft, and they are in every color I can imagine. There are also soft glowing lanterns that look like paper lanterns. Instead of being hung on strings, they just float up and down without being tethered to anything. They look like the lanterns from those festivals where everyone lights a small candle and their lantern floats away. The whole carnival just seems to glow. There are tents of all sizes that look almost exactly like the striped tents from human carnivals. It doesn't have rides like the human carnivals usually have, though. There is no Ferris wheel lighting up the center of the carnival, but it doesn't need one. You can just feel the magic coming from this place. And oh my gods, the smells! I can already smell delicious food.

We pause outside the entrance, still holding hands, and Wold watches me as I stare in awe. Finally I say, "Wold, it's so beautiful."

He smiles at me. Then he checks my antlers and ears to make sure they are in place. To help throw others off the fact that I am human, he asked me to wear my antler headband and my elf ear cuffs. He explained that it won't do anything for my scent, but my scent is so mixed with his, that he hopes it will help me to go unnoticed.

"While we are here, do not leave my side. Do not leave me for anything, Lydia. I am serious about this. You must stay with me at all times."

I nod as I look around in wonder. When he is satisfied that my being human is hidden well enough, he takes my hand again, and we walk through the gate.

Chapter 15

As soon as we are inside the market, I get nervous. I wrap my tail around Lydia's waist. I'm so afraid of something happening to her, and I worry that she does not understand how serious this is. She is so in awe of everything. She has no idea how much danger she could be in.

She gasps and points at all the sights, and it makes me glad to see her smile again. I know we are both sad for her to leave, but I would rather see her happy about this than sad about leaving.

There are so many tents at the market. I haven't been in years, and the market has clearly thrived and grown to almost twice the size it used to be. They have a place where you can buy any kind of spell that you could possibly need, and any kind of ingredient that you could want.

I follow my nose to the tent for mushrooms. As we are walking, Lydia slows down to peek inside any open flap that she sees. There are tents with spices and tents with exotic pets. There are tents for light spells—you can tell which ones those are by the way the tents glow. There are tents for enchanted musical instruments. And tents for plants. You can buy anything your heart desires here. Off to the side, there is a large sinister-looking tent. I don't point it out to Lydia, but it is a tent for pleasure. Anyone can buy pleasure from one of the slaves there. As we head deeper into the market, there are food tents. All of them smell amazing. I should stop and get something with Lydia once we sell some mushrooms and have some coin. I also see clothing tents like what Lydia asked me about. I glance over at her, and I know that she has seen them too. Her smile falters a little at the subtle reminder of what we are going to lose. I pull her to me as we near the mushroom tent. I lean down and ask if she would like some food after we sell the mushrooms.

Her face brightens and she says, "Oh yes! I would love that!" Then she leans into me and whispers, "All the people...they all look so different. Are they all Guardians?"

Just then I look up as a male Guardian walks by. He is a forest Guardian like I am, and he has similar features to me. Except where I am half-Elven, he is not. He is bigger and thicker. His skin resembles dark tree bark, and would feel like tree bark if you touched it. His ears are slightly pointed. Guardians can have a variety of ear types. They range from animalistic ears to ears that are more pointed than a human's, but far less pointed than Elven ears like mine. Only those with Elven blood have long, pointed ears like I do. Instead of having hair like mine, his "hair" is all vines like the ones that are mixed in with my hair. He has huge antlers, much larger than mine. At about his waist, his skin changes from the bark of a tree to the fur of a deer. His feet are cloven hooves, and his legs resemble the hindquarters of a deer. He also has a short deer tail. He has thick muscular arms, and as we watch, he takes a big bite out of a leg of some kind of meat. Goat, maybe?

Lydia's eyes are huge as she watches him walk by. She whispers, "Was that a Guardian?"

"Yes." I feel guilty that I didn't prepare Lydia for this part. I look around at all of the people. They are all Guardians, or half-Guardians like I am. I did not even think about how they would look to Lydia. I watch her as she looks around with wide eyes, then I ask, "Are you okay? Are you afraid?" I'm having trouble catching her exact scent because of all the intermixed scents of the market.

She looks at me startled. "Yes, I'm okay. It's just so much to take in. I'm not afraid. It's just...I don't even know how to describe it. It's amazing." She pauses before continuing, "Do all of these tents sell spells? Can you get any spell you want here?"

I smile at how inquisitive she is. "Probably. A lot of them also sell goods like food or clothing, but even those tents probably also have at least a few spells that they can sell."

We continue walking toward the tent where I can sell the mushrooms. When we get there, I pause outside the tent and say, "When we go in here, just try to be as quiet as possible so that you do not draw attention to yourself. These merchants are not bad, but I do not trust anyone when it comes to you."

She nods in understanding, and we walk into the tent.

I greet the merchant at the back of the tent. This merchant is an older female. She is half-Elven like I am, although her Guardian heritage must have been much different than mine. Where mine pulls traits from the forest, hers seems to be a rockier, mountainous area. Her skin is a stone-gray color and shows the slight texture and pattern of slate. Her hair is a light stone color that is struck through with a lot of silver, but she lacks the vines that grow in my own hair. Her eyes glow a creme color. She has small plants with tiny flowers growing on various spots of her body, like her shoulders and around the base of her neck. They also encircle the two horns on her head. Where my horns resemble the antlers of a deer, hers are the large, thick, coiled horns of a goat. Her feet are the cloven hooves of a mountain goat, and her legs are lightly furred and the same stone color as her skin. She wears a fabric loincloth and has a band of matching fabric tied around her chest to cover her breasts. She also has a long fluffy tail that appears to be rather catlike.

I greet the female and show her the mushrooms that I have to offer. Lydia stands quietly beside me, watching with a look of awe on her face. The merchant buys a large assortment of mushrooms for spells and pays us well with coin.

I thank her and we begin to leave the tent, when Lydia turns back and says, "I love the flowers around your horns. They are beautiful." The merchant gives her a sweet smile and thanks her.

There are a few other types of vendors that I need to seek out, but before that, we need food. I ask Lydia if she is ready to have something to eat. Her face lights up and she says, "Yes! That would be wonderful! Everything smells so good; I'm dying to try something."

We head toward the food tents and find one that has something we both want. I get a leg of roasted deer meat. I haven't hunted deer in a long time, but it is one of my favorite foods. Deer isn't like rabbit, you have to be mindful about how many deer you kill because they do not reproduce quickly.

Lydia gets some type of pastry filled with meat and another one filled with sweet jelly. There are no official dining areas like Lydia is used to, so we look for a large patch of grass at the edge of the market for us to relax and enjoy our food.

We talk and eat every bite of the food we purchased. Lydia even convinces me to try her sweet pastry, which I did not care for. Sweet food just feels wrong to me. It makes me think of meat that has gone bad. Lydia laughs hysterically at the faces of disgust I make while I try to choke down the sweet one.

Once we are done with our food, we relax against a tree. She leans against my chest, and we just watch the magic lights. Everything feels so peaceful at that moment. I'm almost able to forget that I'm about to lose her. Then I remember, and it sucks all the joy out of me. I don't want to let her go. I can't imagine my life without her in it now.

Chapter 16

THE FAE MARKET IS amazing! I love every moment of being here.

There are so many different people. I see Guardians and people that are mixed between Elven and Guardians. They are so fascinating to look at. A lot of them are very similar because they are forest Guardians, but they are also all so different. When you look at the small details of them, you notice all of the little differences that make each person unique. For example, Wold has mushrooms growing on his shoulders and in his hair. I saw another Guardian that was growing lichen, and that one was a female! The merchant that Wold sold mushrooms to was so beautiful. She looked regal and statuesque.

I want to see more.

I want to see everything.

As we've been walking around, I've noticed one female Guardian looking at us on several occasions. I can't figure out why she would be watching us, except maybe she has a thing for Wold? I lean into him because he is mine. Then I realize that after tonight, he won't be, and my heart breaks a little more.

Maybe I shouldn't stand in her way. Maybe Wold would be happy with her. She has the long ears that Wold explained come from being part Elven. Maybe they have similar family histories and could relate to each other. She is also a forest Guardian. She has long green hair, with vines that look a lot like Wold's. She also has antlers that are similar to Wold's, but smaller. Her skin is brown and looks like it has the texture of bark. Her legs are lightly furred, and her paws have a very cat-like look to them. Her tail seems fluffy like a cat's as well. She has a sprinkling of delicate flowers growing on her. Her eyes glow that vibrant yellow like Wold's. She's quite beautiful, really. She's wearing a shimmering piece of fabric that looks like golden silk tied around her small breasts and an elegant loincloth that matches.

I should tell Wold that she is watching us, but I just can't bring myself to point her out to him. Maybe it's jealousy, and I'm not being a good person, but I don't want him to see her and be interested in her. If I can only have him for a little bit longer, I want his whole attention.

So, I don't tell him. He's very busy selling his mushrooms anyway. He doesn't need the distraction. I cling to him though. He still has his tail wrapped around me, and I like the comfort of it.

My heart aches knowing that I am going to lose Wold soon.

We walk around to several more merchants to sell more of the mushrooms.

Before I know it, I look at the bag and realize that all the mushrooms have sold. "Wold! You sold all of them! Did you make a lot of money?"

He smiles. "Yes."

"Did you get enough to buy what you need for the spell?" I ask. Inside I'm pleading to every god I can think of that he didn't.

He looks a little sad as he replies, "Yes, more than enough."

I'm crushed, but I try to put on a smile for him and say, "That's great!" Then I say, "Do we have to...I mean...can we look around a bit more before we buy the ingredients? I love it here, and I want to see more."

He gives me a sad look, yet smiles and says, "Yes, that would be good."

We walk around some more while I marvel at all of the beautiful things the merchants are selling.

We pass a tent, and I peek inside and gasp; it is filled with the most beautiful dresses I have ever seen. There is a beautiful pale pink one that has delicate brown mushrooms embroidered all over it. "Wold, look at that dress! I have to go in and look at it!" He tries to protest, but I practically drag him in.

We walk over to it, and it's even more beautiful up close. I gush over it to Wold. "Look at it! It's perfect!"

A female merchant comes to greet us. She's a forest Guardian too, but she must not have Elven blood. She is much stouter than the females with Elven blood. The ones that are mixed have a much leaner body. She has antlers like most of the forest guardians seem to have, and small flowers bloom around the base of the antlers and around the base of her neck. She asks, "Would you like to try it on?"

I pause and look at Wold, but he looks concerned. He begins darting glances around the tent, so it must not be safe. I look at the merchant and say, "No, I'm just looking." I laugh nervously. "It probably won't fit me; I'm a lot smaller than the females around here."

The merchant smiles. "Nonsense! We use our magic to tailor it to fit you. It would look beautiful with your color, and it would match your mate very well."

I look at Wold again. He looks nervous, and I wouldn't want to cause him any more stress. The merchant notices his concern. "If you are worried about the safety of your woman, do not worry." She takes us to the changing area. "This tent is perfectly safe. We have taken all of the proper precautions and used all the appropriate protection spells for our tent. I have a daughter to protect, and her safety is my top concern. She will just be on the other side of this flap."

She opens a small tent flap and shows us a little dressing room. Wold looks around inside it, and then nods.

The merchant claps and says, "Wonderful! I'll go get the dress." She walks over to the dress display and brings it to us.

I go into the little room and give Wold a big smile. "I'll be out in just a minute." He still looks nervous, but he nods.

Once I've closed the flap for the dressing room, I take my clothes off except for my bra and panties. I slip the dress on and button it up the front. As soon as I put it on, I feel the fabric shrinking to fit me, and I gasp. It fits perfectly, and it's so soft and lightweight. I twirl, because you have to twirl in a new flowy dress.

I hear a sound like shuffling feet coming from the opposite side of the dressing room, not the flap where I entered. This makes me nervous, because why would I hear someone walking around there? I feel like I'm being watched, and my heart starts racing. Maybe Wold was right; maybe this is too dangerous. I decide I want to get out of here and get back to Wold as quickly as possible, so I begin gathering up my clothes. I hear a noise behind me, and I whirl around. The female that has been watching us pokes her head through a hidden flap in the dressing room. I gasp. "You—"

She cuts me off with a whisper, "I'm sorry for this." She blows a handful of dust into my face.

I cough as it goes into my mouth and nose. I don't feel right. I feel weak and dizzy. I look at the female again, and then I collapse as everything goes dark.

Chapter 17

I WAIT OUTSIDE THE little *dressing room*, as Lydia called it. I am very stressed about being separated, even this much. I know she is just on the other side of this flap, and is safe, but I just cannot turn off the fear of something happening to her.

I hear a faint noise that sounds like a gasp from Lydia. I step closer to the flap to listen.

Just then, the merchant comes to my side. "Is there anything else you would like to look at for your woman?"

I notice that she keeps referring to Lydia as a 'woman' instead of a female. She must know that Lydia is human. Instantly my heart drops and I have a sinking feeling in my stomach. Something is happening.

The merchant is still speaking as my mind races with panic. "We have this lovely, flavored body powder that is great for intimate..." Then she blows a puff of powder in my face. I sneeze and shake my head...then I realize...

I rasp, "No!" Then I collapse as everything goes dark.

***

When I wake, the sun is rising. My head is pounding and even the smallest amount of light sears my eyes.

I blink rapidly, trying to figure out what happened and where I am. This isn't my home, and Lydia isn't curled up next to me...

Oh gods, Lydia!

I remember what happened now. I get up as quickly as I am able, and stagger to the *dressing room*. I rip open the flap with my claws.

Lydia isn't there.

I can barely scent her, but my head is full of the smell of whatever they used to drug me. Her bag and clothes are lying there on the floor, and on the other side of the room, another flap is open.

There was a second way in.

Lydia is gone.

Someone took her.

My sweet little sprite.

My heart starts racing, and I hear the blood pounding in my ears. My muscles burn with the urge to destroy whoever took her. I bellow in anger and begin tearing through everything while screaming Lydia's name. I'm desperate to find some small hint of where she was taken.

It doesn't take me long to completely destroy the clothing and the tent. I'm standing in the shreds of what is left.

Most customers have left already, but there are still merchants there, and many of them are coming out of their tents now to see what the noise is.

A few curious merchants are watching me, but most quickly look away and continue what they were doing. I yell, "Lydia!! Did anyone see where they took her?" A few people shake their heads.

Just then I catch a faint thread of Lydia's scent. It is mixed with the scent of two females. One is the dress merchant, and the other is similar, but younger.

I roar with rage. Then I spring out of the tent wreckage and run as hard as I can chasing Lydia's scent. The scent is so faint that she must have been taken hours ago. Please, gods, let me find her.

I race across the ground until I get to the woods, and then I spring from tree to tree. It is faster than running along the ground, and it will allow me a good vantage point when I do get to her.

Lydia, I am coming for you.

Chapter 18

I GROAN AS I wake up, eyes crusted shut. Oh gods, I feel awful. My head is pounding, and my stomach feels terrible.

What happened? I remember the market. I remember eating the pies. The pretty Guardian that I didn't like. That dress and the creepy dressing room. I gasp...THAT PRETTY GUARDIAN!

Wold! Where is Wold?

I try to move, but my stomach is roiling, and I fight the urge to vomit up those wonderful tasting pies from earlier.

There is a slight bouncing or vibrating feeling to whatever I'm in. Also, whatever I am laying on is prickly and causing me to itch. I crack an eye open and realize that I'm lying on hay. There is also a clomping sound, like horse hooves. I crack the other eye open and vaguely look around.

It's a cart. I'm in a cart.

I shift a little so I can look up. It's covered with something, some kind of thick cloth.

Oh gods, I feel so bad. What was that stuff she blew in my face? Who was that female? I roll over as I vomit. I purge everything out of my stomach, then I crawl away from the mess. At least there is hay in here to absorb it, I would hate to end up lying in it. I snort a tiny sarcastic laugh. I guess it's the small things that count right now.

I lay there as my situation sinks in. I've been kidnapped. Oh gods. This is exactly what Wold was worried about. Now I realize just how right he was to be worried. I only went to the market for one night, and someone kidnapped me.

I manage to prop myself up a little and I try to peek between the cloth covering and the wood of the side of the cart. I can see sunlight, so it must be daytime.

I remember the mushrooms Wold gave me, and I decide to take one now. It may be a little early for it, but I would rather be safe than sorry. And I have no idea how late in the day it is. I cough and gag as I try to swallow it, but I manage to get it down without getting sick again. I'm counting that as a win.

I lay there for a long time just trying to figure out what to do. How am I going to get away? I can barely even move without vomiting. I finally decide that I will just have to wait for an opportunity to come up. I'll have to play along with this kidnapping and see where it goes. Oh man, I'm not even sure if this counts as a plan. I can't do anything while I am this weak, so I will just have to rest and wait for now.

I doze in the hay for hours. I peek out under the cloth and see that the sun has started setting. We've been traveling all day. How far is that in a wagon? Certainly it's miles and miles. Oh gods, what am I going to do?

At least I'm feeling a little bit better and don't feel like I'm going to vomit anymore. And I may feel a little stronger. That's hard to judge without being able to stand up, though. My head is still pounding, and the light hurts my eyes.

The cart comes to a stop, and I'm instantly on alert. I hear people walking around to the back of the cart, so I crawl away from them.

I hear a man's voice. It sounds almost musical, but not at all friendly. He yells at someone to let him see what they brought him.

Oh gods. It's me. I'm what they brought him. Thoughts of what Wold's birth mother did to his father race through my head.

A female voice says, "We were able to take her from the market last night. I think you will be pleased with her."

The man snaps at her, "I better, or you know what the cost will be."

Someone pulls up the cloth covering on the back portion of the cart and gasps. Then I am staring wide-eyed at the most beautiful man I have ever seen. His skin and hair look like gold, actual gold. He even shimmers a little. It makes him look otherworldly. He turns his head, and I see his long elegant, pointed ears. He must be Elven.

Oh no.

He looks at the female. "A human! How did *you* manage to find a human?"

The female replies, "A Guardian brought her to the market."

The man scrunches his face in disgust and cups his hand over his nose. "A Guardian? That must be why she reeks of dirty seed."

I hear a small gasp from a younger-sounding female. Then I hear the original female tut before she says, "She is quite lovely, sir. Once she is cleaned up, it will only be a matter of days before she quits smelling of his seed."

Did he really say dirty seed?! He's the disgusting one, not Wold.

The man laughs. "I know that. I am only disappointed that I will have to wait a few days to play with my lovely new toy."

Oh no, no no no no. This can't be happening. He's going to keep me as a plaything just like Wold's birth mother did to males. My heart is racing, a high-pitched ringing sounds in my ears, and I start breathing heavily. Think, Lydia, think. You still have a few days before he will touch you.

I hear the female say, "Sir, I think you are frightening her. I can smell her fear."

The impossibly beautiful man looks at me again. Even his eyes are gold. His long shimmering hair is tied back at the nape of his neck. The tunic he wears is elaborate and speaks volumes of his wealth. It looks like it's made from cream-colored silk and has golden embroidery. He smiles at me, displaying dangerous fangs. "Do not worry, kitten. You will enjoy every moment of your time with me. You will be begging for more."

Oh gods. He's going to glamour me. He's actually going to try and glamour me! Thank the gods Wold gave me those mushrooms. I hope they really work.

The man stares at me again. He gives me a strange, very intense look. "Don't worry, we will get to my estate and clean you up. Then we will have a delicious dinner together. You will see. It will be wonderful." He gives me that malicious smile again.

Wait. Is he trying to glamour me now? Huh, those mushrooms must really work. But in order to stay safe, I have to play along, so I take in a slow, deep breath, then I smile and nod at him. This seems to appease him. He smiles back, then shuts the cloth covering. I hear him say to the female, "I am surprised, but you did well. Let us go back to my estate and we will discuss the terms of our agreement."

"Thank you, sir."

A few minutes later, the cart starts moving again.

Chapter 19

I FURIOUSLY CHASE LYDIA'S scent all day. The sun begins to set, and my body is exhausted. I can't stop moving though. If I lose her scent or the other females' scents, then I will lose her forever. I must keep up with the scent.

A little after dark, I reach a place on the road where her scent is much stronger and lingers more. I catch threads of fear intertwined with her normal smell. There are new scents in the mix now; the one that worries me the most is a male scent. An Elven scent. I roar with rage.

I climb back into the trees and leap my way after her. I can see now that she must have been hidden in a cart. That's why her scent was so faint. She wasn't touching anything outside of the cart, so her scent remained contained. The females that took her must have known I would hunt her down, and they were trying their best to keep Lydia's scent hidden.

They must have met the Elven male here, and I'm guessing he wanted to see what they brought him, so he uncovered Lydia for a couple of minutes. Long enough to let enough of her scent drift onto the wind.

Now I know exactly what I'm hunting. Even if I lose her scent, I have his scent and the horses' scents. I have cart tracks and hoof tracks.

I will find her, and I will rescue her. I will not allow her to be taken as a prisoner like so many others.

Gods, I hope she remembers to take the mushrooms that I gave her. She placed them in the clothing that holds her breasts. I can't remember what it is called right now, and I've thought that it was the dumbest piece of clothing ever invented. But now I am thanking the gods for those silly little scraps of cloth. It means that she should still have the mushrooms, unless they took her clothes. That thought causes ice to run through my veins.

There are ways to break the glamour if the Elven has glamoured her. I will stop at nothing to get her back healthy and whole. I will break any spell that he has cast on her.

I chase her scent well into the night, and it eventually leads me to a lavish estate. I can see where the cart tracks enter the front gate.

Now that I am here, I recognize this place.

This is my birth mother's estate.

***

Lydia

The rest of the cart trip feels like it takes forever. I think it must have been a couple of hours, but with no way to tell time, I have no idea. It could have been two hours, or it could have been thirty minutes.

I feel the cart slowing to a stop and hear more voices outside. I hear something large moving with a heavy scraping sound, maybe a gate of some sort? We must be at the Elven's estate.

I hear his voice; he's barking orders to others. Gods, how am I going to get myself out of this?

After a few shouted instructions, the cart starts moving again. I curl up in the hay and try not to panic. I have no idea what's waiting for me here. They mentioned cleaning me up, so maybe a bath?

I wish I were with Wold. I wonder if they drugged him like they drugged me. I hope he's okay.

I hope he is looking for me.

The cart comes to a stop, pulling me from my thoughts about Wold. I hear people talking. I hear the females from earlier.

Someone pulls back the fabric covering the cart, and I'm suddenly looking into the faces of several people. One of those people is the female I saw following Wold and I at the market. I gasp and say, "You! You did this!?"

Then I see the other female guardian. She's the merchant from the dress shop. The one that was pushing me to try on the dress. I gasp and point a finger at her, "You were in on this too?! All of that pushing to get me to try on this dress was so you could kidnap me? Where is Wold? What did you do to him?" I'm yelling at her by this point, and she just gives me a wry smile.

"If you know what is good for you, you will hush right now, woman."

This just enrages me more, so I yell louder. "I will not hush. You drugged me and kidnapped me!"

A cold, melodic voice cuts in from the other side of the room. "Well, I see that this little kitten is a feisty one." The Elven male is leaning in a doorway watching all of this unfold. "That's okay, I like feisty females. They take a little extra taming, but it is worth it. I will have you purring for me in no time."

I glare at him. I want to yell and scream and throw things, but I don't want to push him. I know deep down that he is depending on being able to glamour me, and I do not want him to discover that I can't be glamoured. Hopefully I'm right, and he was trying to glamour me earlier because that means the mushrooms work. I don't even want to think about what it means if I'm wrong.

He says, "Aww, don't be angry, kitten. I promise I will take good care of you. You will want for nothing." He saunters toward me. "Let's get you cleaned up, and then we can have a nice dinner and get to know each other."

He snaps his fingers twice, and two Elven females quickly come over and bow before him. They are not quite as fantastical looking as him—he practically looks like a golden god—but they still look beautiful in an otherworldly way. They both have deep burnt orange skin and hair, and seem to emit an ethereal glow. It reminds me of something, but I can't quite place it. I study them for a few moments. I notice the way the light shimmers off them. Suddenly it hits me what they remind me of.

When my mother was still alive, she always wore a pendant. It was a simple pendant with a stone set in silver, but the stone was beautiful. It was a dark orange and flashed like fire when the light hit it. I loved looking at it when I was little. I would sit in my mother's lap and play with it while she told me the story of where it came from. I could turn it in different directions to catch the light and see the little flashes of fire within it. I was so mesmerized by the stone, that I missed most of what she said. I was never good at listening when I was a child, but I remember that it was my grandmother's from before my grandmother was sent far away from her home to marry a wealthy man that she didn't know. My mother inherited it when my grandmother died, and then my mother passed it on to me. I've always been too afraid to wear it. I was so afraid I would lose it, that I put it in a safe deposit box at the bank before I moved away from the city.

The Elven male snaps me out of my thoughts when he says, "Take this woman to her rooms, draw her a bath, and make her presentable for dinner."

Then he turns and walks off. I'm left standing in the cart, glaring at the two females from the market. The two Elven servants walk over to the cart. One of them says, "Come, we will take you to bathe."

I glare at them for a minute, too. I want to fight. I want to tell them no and to fuck off. But I suspect that will only draw attention from the one that wants me as his plaything. I think it will be in my best interest to play nice and not cause any problems until I can figure out a way to escape from here.

I jump down from the cart.

The one that spoke says, "Follow us." Then they turn and start walking. I follow them through a doorway.

The two female Guardians, the ones that kidnapped me, stay behind in the garage or whatever you would call it.

The doorway that we go through leads straight into the most opulent foyer that I have ever seen. I gasp as we walk in. I feel like I have just walked into a palace. Maybe I have. This Elven is obviously wealthy and powerful, so he must have some sort of title. Everything is gilded in gold or covered in silk. I momentarily forget my situation and murmur, "Wow, look at this place."

The two servants look at me, but don't say anything.

We turn right out of the foyer and walk down a long corridor that is just as extravagant as the entryway. Along the corridor, there are golden statues of women in different poses. At the end, we turn right again and enter a luxurious suite.

Chapter 20

THE BED IN THE suite is huge. It's a four-poster bed with silk curtains. Just like the other rooms, everything is gilded gold or silk covered. There's even a golden statue of a woman in here as well.

There is a bathroom off to the side, and in it is a gold clawfoot tub. There's also a toilet; well, not really a toilet—it's one of the old-style primitive kind that's basically a hole in a seat. Considering I have been peeing in the woods for a few days, it seems luxurious.

As I take in everything in the room, one of the servants goes over to the wall beside the tub and lowers a panel in the wall. A golden pipe springs out and is aimed directly at the tub. The servant rings a small bell twice. I hear a gurgling sound, and suddenly steamy water is running out of the pipe.

I gasp. "How?"

"There is a stream that runs under the estate," one of the servants says. "Our Lord has a Water Guardian there that controls the water. He heats the water and sends it up the pipes when it's needed for a bath."

All I say is, "Oh." I don't really want to be friendly with these servants. I also feel pretty certain that the Water Guardian that heats the bath water isn't doing this of his own free will. So I just watch as the tub fills up. The servants add different soaps and oils to the water, and a mountain of sweet-scented bubbles form in the tub.

One of the servants looks at me. "You can get undressed now and get in the tub."

I take my filthy dress off. It's still the one from that merchant's tent, the one that got me into this mess. I'm standing there in my bra and panties, and the servants are looking at me expectantly. I can't just take my bra off because I have the mushrooms tucked into it. I put on my shyest expression and ask them if I can have some privacy to relieve myself and get in the tub.

One of the servants says, "Yes, just call out when you are ready for us to come help you." Then they go into the bedroom—I'm assuming to get a dress ready for me to wear to dinner with Lord asshole tonight.

What am I going to do?

I actually did need to pee really bad, so I use the toilet. There were two baskets beside the toilet. One had a fresh pile of folded linens in it, and the other was completely empty. After staring at it for a few minutes, I decide that the linens are for wiping and the empty basket is for the used ones.

There are large decorative vases around the bathroom. I hide my little bag of mushrooms in one of the vases, then I slip my bra and panties off and get into the tub.

Loudly I say, "You can come back."

The two servants come back into the room and get to work trying to bathe me. It startles me at first and I try to do it myself, but they ignore my protests. They are determined to help clean and moisturize my hair and scrub every inch of my body. So eventually I give up fighting them and follow their instructions. I stand up when they tell me to and rinse off when they tell me to. Once I am thoroughly bathed, they tell me to stand and get out of the tub. Then they proceed to dry me off with a big fluffy towel.

Once I am dried off to their liking, I am allowed to wrap up in the towel, and we go into the bedroom. However, once we are in there, they take the towel from me. Then they rub different oils and perfumes all over my body.

Next, they dress me in what looks like a simple cotton nightgown or slip, but must be some sort of underwear for the dress they have laid out for me. They have me put on fancy-looking boots next. That is followed by a corset that makes me look amazing but feels awful. Then they top it all off with the most elaborate dress I have ever seen. My hair is swept up into a sophisticated-looking updo and adorned with elegant jewels. And then, they are done.

I stand in front of the mirror for a few minutes just staring at myself. This is easily the most beautiful I have ever looked, but I'm so miserable. I can see it written all over my face. I want out of this awful place. I want to be with Wold.

How did all of this turn into such a mess? Will Wold come after me?

Oh gods, I suddenly remember what this Elven's plans are for me. Oh gods, is he going to expect sex tonight? Will I be able to do that? Will I be able to suffer through and fake it? I don't want this. I don't want any of this. Is this going to be what my life is like from now on? Pretty dresses and fancy baths, followed by fancy dinners, then forcing myself to have sex with that horrible... male?

The thought of him touching me, Gods, I can't do that. I begin trembling. I feel like I can't catch my breath, and I hear my breathing get heavier. This stupid corset, I can't breathe with this stupid corset on. I begin pulling at the dress, desperately trying to figure out a way to loosen it so I can breathe. One of the servants notices my anxiety and must realize the source. She gently takes both of my hands in hers. "Calm yourself, woman. Our Lord only wants dinner and conversation from you tonight. He will wait until you no longer smell of the Guardian before he takes you to his bed. He will satisfy himself with...others until he is able to have you."

Relief floods through me. But then I realize what she just said. "He has others? Other women or female guests?"

She averts her eyes and shakes her head. "No, no other guests. He will choose from..." The other servant gives her a look to silence her, and she trails off without finishing the sentence. I understand though. He will choose from his servants. Probably one of these two females will have to go to bed with him. The horror of it settles into me. Gods, this is awful.

"Can I at least know what his name is?" I ask.

The servant says, "It's Lord Varik. But he will not want you to use his name. Just say 'my lord' to him."

"Okay. How long will it take for the scent to be gone?" I feel like I have a knot in my throat just from thinking about this.

The servant looks at me and shrugs. "Probably a few days."

A few days, that's all I have. Oh gods. I have to figure out how to get out of here.

Chapter 21

I PACE OUTSIDE THE walls of the estate. I am sure to stay hidden from the Elven guards that I see.

My birth mother's estate. I cannot believe that Lydia's kidnapping has brought me back here to this horrible home. Is this all for my birth mother? Is she still alive? That is not something I have worried about since I was a child.

It doesn't matter if my birth mother is a part of this. It changes nothing. I will still break into the estate and rescue Lydia. It doesen't matter who tries to stand in my way.

I hear noises from the front gate.

I silently stalk my way over to a nearby tree and watch to see what the noise is. It's a cart leaving. The back of the cart is uncovered but I am able to scent that Lydia was in it. This is the cart that carried her here. I can also scent that she vomited in the cart, and I growl. The two female scents that stole her are driving the cart. Rage burns through me that these females would dare to take her.

I leap from tree to tree until I have caught up with the cart, then I leap into the back of it. I immediately grab the older of the two females and throw her to the ground. I jump down on top of her and pin her by her throat. My claws dig in and little rivulets of blood run from the wounds and drip to the dirt under her. The other female is screaming. I am growling and snarling at this point.

I am made of rage. I roar in the older female's face, and the other female begs me not to kill her. But I will not let these two live. They will pay for this with their lives.

I snarl. "Where is she? Where is my mate?"

The female that I have pinned down gasps and chokes as she tries to respond to me. I loosen my grip on her throat just a small bit. She coughs as she says, "Please, don't kill her. Do what you want to me, but don't kill my daughter."

Daughter? I look to the younger female that is cowering by the cart. That explains why their scents were so similar.

I snarl again. "Your fate is not up for debate. Where is my mate?"

The mother begs again, and tears are rolling off of her face. "Please...please have mercy on us. He took her...he took my daughter." She chokes on a sob. "He forced her into his bed. He told me he would sell her to the highest bidder if I did not find someone better." She gasps and coughs. "He wanted...someone that wasn't a dirty Guardian."

I look to her daughter. She is on the ground on her knees and openly weeping now. I can scent the male on her and I growl. Lydia wouldn't want me to hurt these two females.

"Please, I only took her so that he would let my daughter go." She chokes again and sobs. "I'm sorry. I had to save my daughter."

I yank her up off the ground and shove her toward the cart. She stumbles and falls near her daughter. Her daughter crawls to her side and holds her.

"I should spill your blood for what you stole from me, but she would not want me to hurt you. That is the only reason you are still alive. Now tell me where she is."

The mother is still gasping and sobbing. "Thank you, sir...thank you...thank you."

I roar, "Tell me where my mate is!"

"He took her. He wanted her cleaned up so that they could dine together," she says between sobs. "He said he would not have her in his bed while she smelled of dirty Guardian seed." She gasps for breath. "You yet have time to help her. It should take a few days for your scent to wear off."

"Take your cart and go. Never come back to this place."

Both females climb up onto the cart as quickly as they can and leave.

Chapter 22

WHILE I CIRCLE THE perimeter of the estate, I remember a gate in the wall that my nursemaid would use to sneak me out of the estate so that I could run free and play without worrying about my birth mother seeing me. I remember that the lock on it was broken. I only have a vague memory of where it is, but I follow the wall and hunt for it or any other hidden entrance into the estate.

I head to the backside of the estate. Once I am behind it, I run into overgrown vines and plants. Excellent cover for me. I make my way through them.

Near the heart of the plant life, I find the old gate. It's dirty from the elements and the plants, but there's still the gilded gleam of the metal in certain spots. Vines are tangled through the gate, so I have to break it free before I can open it.

It creaks open and I slip in. I stay hidden within the vines for a few minutes to make sure that no one was drawn by the noise of the gate. Once I'm certain that no one is coming, I creep onto the estate grounds.

Being back here brings a flood of memories back from when my nursemaid was raising me. My birth mother had been horrible, but my time with my nursemaid was fun.

The building closest to the gate is the servant quarters. I make my way towards it.

As I creep behind it, I catch a scent from one of the open windows. It stops me in my tracks. I know that scent. It's engrained in all my earliest memories. Nanni. Is she still here?

I follow the scent to the open window, and peek inside. I can hear voices, but not well enough to tell if it is her. One of the voices sounds like a child's voice.

I wait at the window, hoping to see someone.

A child runs across the room and stops while still in view of the window. She's a female Guardian. She has Elven ears and build, and her Guardian traits seem very similar to mine. Too similar to be a coincidence.

She must be another child from my birth mother and father.

I'm unable to look away as that realization sinks in. I'd never considered that I would ever have a family, but I know that my birth mother did not let my father go free, so she would have had ample opportunities to become pregnant by him again.

The child turns and looks at me. She goes still when she sees me peering in the window.

For a moment, I am frozen and do not know what to do.

Then, a female Guardian steps into view. She has her back to me, but I know this is Nanni just from seeing her back. She is half-Elven like I am, but her skin is a dark mottled brown. Her legs are lightly furred like a deer, and end in delicate hooves. I can't see it, but I know she has a short, fluffy tail similar to a deer as well. Her hair is long and brown, with green vines growing through it. Her antlers are lighter than mine, and she has soft yellow flowers growing around the base of them and on the tops of her shoulders. She wears a strip of brown silk fabric tied around her chest to cover her small breasts. She has also wrapped and tied a strip of the same fabric around her hips to form a skirt.

I whisper, "Nanni."

She turns, and when she sees me in the window, she gasps. "Wold."

Then she motions for me to stay where I am. She grabs the child's hand and they quickly walk out the front door, then come around to the back of the building where I am.

She reaches up to put both of her hands on my cheeks like she used to when I was small. Then with tears her in eyes, she says, "Oh Wold. Look at you. You've grown up."

I smile and say, "Nanni." Then I step towards her, open my arms, and wrap them around her the way that Lydia does to me. She startles and freezes for a moment but recovers quickly. Her eyes dart around us, then she whispers, "What are you doing here? You can't be here. You must leave."

I give her a dark look and say, "They have my mate."

Nanni gasps and covers her mouth. "The woman that everyone has been talking about? Is she in the main house?"

"I do not know where she is. I am hunting her scent. They took her from the market and brought her back here. I followed her scent here."

"That must be the woman everyone has been talking about. The staff has spoken of nothing else tonight. The servants were getting her prepared for dinner with Lord Varik." Nanni says.

I growl. "Who is Lord Varik? Is my birth mother not the lady of this estate?"

Nanni gives me a sad look. Then she says, "Wold, your mother died almost five years ago. Varik is her son...your half-brother. He is the lord of the estate now."

I just stare at Nanni. I finally say, "How?"

"One of the Guardians...the ones that your mother held as prisoners. One of them killed her. She went into his cage one night, for her...activities, and he killed her. Her glamour over him must not have held. Glamours don't work as well on Guardians, and maybe he grew to resist it."

"Good." I have known how cruel my birth mother was for my entire life; I would never mourn her death. I am glad that whichever Guardian it was that killed her was able to get his revenge.

Nanni gives me a cautious look, then gestures to the child that has been quietly watching us. "Wold...this is Pampa. She's your sister. Most likely by the same Guardian."

With that, Pampa steps forward and softly says, "Hello."

I reply, "Hello, I am Wold." I look to Nanni. "I have to get Lydia out."

Nanni smiles. "Let us help you."

***

Nanni's plan is to sneak up to the main house while Lord Varik is at dinner with Lydia. Lydia's rooms should be empty at this time. Pampa will sneak into Lydia's room and unlock one of the large windows so I can crawl in and hide until the servants leave Lydia for the night. Then I can come out of hiding and rescue Lydia by crawling back through the window. If all goes well, we should be able to sneak back off the estate grounds the same way that I came in.

Chapter 23

THE TWO SERVANTS TAKE me to a grand dining room. If I thought the entryway and bedroom were extravagant, they are nothing compared to the dining room. Everything is gilded and shines. There is a long table with so much food laid out that it resembles a buffet for a huge party. Orbs of magic light float above the table and are scattered throughout the room. It makes the space look magical.

At the other end of the room is a large golden table, and sitting at the head of it is Lord Varik. He stands when we enter the room, then walks toward me and says, "There now, kitten, don't you look lovely. You cleaned up very well."

He reaches for my hand, and my first reaction is to step back from him. When I do, I see a dark look cross his face.

Then he begins giving me a strange look. He's intentional-
ly looking me in the eye and holding my gaze. He must be
trying to glamour me, so I feign that it's working. I smile
sweetly and say, "Thank you, my lord."

His face relaxes and he takes my hand and kisses my
palm. Keeping a hold on my hand, he guides me toward the
table where he had been sitting. As I approach the table, I
count the chairs. There's twelve of them. All but two of
them have statues sitting in the chairs. Gleaming, golden
statues. They are in various poses that make it look like
they are enjoying a dinner party. One of them even has a
golden fork raised to its mouth as if it's about to take a bite
of something delicious. Lord Varik draws my attention
away from the statues when he says, "I'm so glad you could
join me for dinner tonight." He pulls out a chair for me
and tells me to sit.

I sit like the good girl I'm pretending to be. I try to be
all sweet smiles on the outside even though I am all rage
and disgust on the inside. How many women or females
has he done this to? How many people has he glamoured
and forced into doing something that they didn't want
to? I wonder if you remember everything while you are
glamoured...

He pours a dark wine out of a bottle and into two
sparkling crystal and gold glasses. He sets one in front of

me, then he says, "Now, dear kitten, tell me, how are your rooms? Are they to your liking?"

I smile vapidly and say, "Oh yes, my lord. They are perfect." Then I go back to sitting quietly in my spot.

He gives me a wolfish grin. "Good. How about we eat? You must be starving after that dreadful wagon ride. I hope you know that I meant nothing bad by it. I just needed a way to get you here. It was merely a little bit of suffering that you needed to endure to make the later pleasures all that much better."

Without thinking, I say, "Oh."

He gives me a slight frown. "I do hope that you don't hold that against me, kitten."

I smile more brightly and say, "Of course not. You were only doing what was best for me."

That seems to appease him. "Let us eat." He picks up a small golden bell and rings it to signal to the two servants, and I have to fight to keep from rolling my eyes. Seriously, a bell? The two females were still in the room, he could have just said he was ready to eat. The two servants walk over to the table of food and each pick up a large, heavy-looking platter and bring them to the table. The lord points to the foods that he wants, and they put it on his plate. One of the servants looks at me expectantly and I point to a couple of foods that look mild and like I might be able to stomach them. They then carry the large platters back to the table. Once they have deposited their platters, they stand on each end of the table, waiting to be called upon again.

We eat mostly in silence. Lord Varik doesn't seem to be all that concerned with making small talk, and I'm not sure if someone that was under an Elven glamour would talk a lot. Somehow, I doubt it, so I decide staying quiet is the safest idea.

I make it through dinner, and then Lord Varik wants to take me on a tour of his home. All of it is just as extravagant as everything else I have seen. I try to gasp and feign awe at all the appropriate times.

There are several sitting rooms. There is a huge ballroom complete with a large staircase and balcony that looks exactly like what you would expect in some kind of princess story.

All of the rooms have at least a few of those same strange golden statues. They are all posed as if they are enjoying a party. It's a bit creepy. I guess if he can't make real friends, he can buy some golden ones.

He leads me to a large corridor and explains that his rooms are down there, and I am not to go to his wing of the house. Yeah...he doesn't really need to worry about that. I'm definitely going to stay as far away from him as possible.

He goes on to explain, "Once you no longer smell of…that Guardian, I will come visit you in your quarters. And if you find you are suddenly in need of me, you can always send one of the servants." I smile at him as one of the female servants appears at my side.

"Now, if you will excuse me, I have something I must…attend to before I retire for the night. It has been a lovely evening, and I look forward to spending tomorrow with you. Maybe I can take you on a tour of the grounds." He lifts my hand and kisses my palm again. "The servant will return you to your room."

I try not to shudder at the weird palm kiss. Why would he kiss my palm instead of the back of my hand?

I thank him, and then he strolls down his corridor to his rooms. Gods only know what he has to run off to do. I'm just grateful that he's leaving me alone for the rest of the night.

The servant says, "Come, follow me." Then she leads me back to my room. Once we are there, she takes out a nightgown and robe and helps me get undressed. She asks me if I would like another bath. I just shake my head no. I just want her to leave. While I'm changing into the nightgown, I try to think about what I'm going to do. I have to find my way out of this horrible place as soon as I can. My room has large windows that overlook the patio, hopefully I can slip out one of those during the night.

I vaguely notice that the servant is pouring something into her hand. She walks over to me and says, "I'm so sorry." Then she blows a familiar powder in my face.

"Oh...shit..." I collapse into darkness.

Chapter 24

Earlier while Lydia is at dinner.

There are tunnels that lead from the servant's quarters to the main house.

Nanni and Pampa lead me through the tunnels and show me where they lead into the house. It's a corridor just outside of the kitchen. Pampa sneaks into the hallway and quietly runs down the corridor and takes a left at the end of it. Nanni has me stay just inside the tunnel with her. We shut the door and wait.

If everything goes according to plan, we will wait here while Pampa sneaks into Lydia's room and unlocks one of the less conspicuous windows. Once that is done, Pampa will sneak back to the servant tunnels and meet us just inside. Then the three of us will head back down the tunnels to the servant quarters. From there, I will creep up to the house and slip into the unlocked window in Lydia's room. I will hide away there and wait until the servants are gone. Once we are alone, I will get Lydia and escape through the unlocked window.

While we are waiting, Nanni looks at me and says, "I am so glad I've gotten to see you again tonight. It was so hard to leave you…" She puts her hand on my arm. "You are like a son to me. It broke my heart when your mother made me leave you and return here. Please know that I have missed you every day since then."

I clasp my hand around hers, and say, "I always considered you my mother, and I've missed you very much. I wanted to make you proud of me and be the best Guardian I could be. But what my land demands of me, it took its toll. It made me feel like a monster…the monster that my birth mother always said I was. I hid away and lived like an animal. It wasn't until Lydia showed up that I felt like a person again."

Nanni gives me a sad look.

"I want Lydia to stay with me. She wants to stay with me. She thinks we are meant to be together. She has begged to stay with me, but I was going to send her home so that she would be safe. We went to the market to get supplies to do the spell that opens the barrier so that she could go back through. That's where they kidnapped her." I give Nanni a hopeless look. "I tried to keep her safe as best as I could, but I couldn't protect her. I still want her to stay with me, but a human isn't safe in our world. Sending her home is going to break me, I can feel it. I will turn back into the monster again."

Nanni pats my arm and says, "Maybe Lydia is right, and you are meant to be together. If you give her your mating bite, she will be bound to you."

"They could still just take her again. She's a human, the Elven will always want her." I argue.

"Not if you give her your mating bite. The magic will bind your souls together and change her. She won't be human anymore." Nanni explains.

Hope begins to bloom in my chest, and I ask, "What do you mean she won't be human? Will she be a Guardian?"

"No, not Guardian or Elven. With humans, the magic changes them into something different. Something human, but also fae," Nanni explains. "I have seen a human that was mated to a Guardian once. She still looked a lot like a human, but she had fae magic and fae features. Her ears were pointed like yours and she carried some of the features of her mate. She had curved horns like his."

"But how would that keep her safe if someone else wanted to take her as their plaything?" I ask.

"The bond. You would always be connected to each other. You would know exactly how to find her. It would keep her safe. No one is going to try to steal someone that has a mating bond. It's a death wish."

I don't know what to say. We could have avoided all of this. I give Nanni a helpless look and I say, "I did not know...there is so much I do not know."

She pats my arm again. "Oh Wold, I'm so sorry. There was so much I needed to teach you, and I had such little time to do it. I had to focus on what you needed to survive, and not on things like mating bonds."

"I do not blame you." I say. "You did the best you could with the time you had."

We are quiet for a moment, and then I say, "Shouldn't Pampa be back by now?"

Nanni has a worried look on her face. "Yes, I didn't expect it would take this long. We will give her a little longer, and if she is not back, then I will try to slip over there and find out what is happening."

Something must have gone wrong.

A few minutes later, we hear a commotion in the corridor leading up to the servant's tunnel. It's Pampa. I can hear her pleading with someone.

She's saying, "I just wanted to see her. Everyone is talking about her, and I wanted to see what she looks like.

Please don't tell Nanni, she will be angry with me. I promise I won't try to spy on her again."

I give Nanni a look, then step back into the shadows of the tunnel. Nanni steps out of the tunnel and shuts the door. I hear her say in a scolding tone, "Pampa! There you are! I've been looking for you! What are you doing here? You know we aren't supposed to be in the main house right now!"

Another female voice says, "It seems this little one got curious about the new woman that our lord brought home. I've already scolded her and told her to stay out of here. Fortunately, no harm was done. She should be glad it was me that found her and not Lord Varik."

Pampa pleads, "I'm so sorry Nanni! I just wanted to see if she is as beautiful as everyone said. I've never seen a human. I promise I won't do it again."

Nanni says, "Thank you, I will take care of her from here. Come, Pampa, we need to go back to our room, and then we are going to have a talk about this." Then she shoos Pampa into the tunnel.

Once both of them are in the tunnel, Nanni gestures for us to be quiet until she is certain that the servant left. Then she asks Pampa what happened.

Pampa looks at us with huge, worried eyes, and says, "I couldn't get the window unlocked. I went into the room, but before I could unlock the window, I scented one of the servants coming. I hid in the closet, but she must have scented me, and she found me. Nanni, I think..." She gives me a nervous look then continues, "I don't think this is going to work. The servant was in there putting a heavy chain and cuff on the bedpost. I think they are going to cuff her to the bed."

"What?!" Rage consumes me.

Nanni strokes my arm and shushes me. "Wold, calm yourself. Anger will not help us right now. If he is going to chain her to the bed, then he thinks that she will try to run. We need to come up with another plan."

I growl.

Nanni tuts at me. "Let us go back to our room and think of another plan."

Chapter 25

I DO NOT SLEEP at all that night. I pace the floor like a caged animal. Late in the night, after Pampa goes to sleep, I sneak up to the house to see if I can peer into one of Lydia's windows. There are guards patrolling the main house, but I manage to slip by them and get to one of the side windows of her room.

I see her asleep on her bed. Pampa was right; I can see a cuff on her ankle. They have her chained to the bed. I'm filled with rage that they would dare do this to her, but I quickly try to rein it in before I break the window in front of me. I test the window to see if it might be unlocked, but it's not. I go around to each window in her room and test them all one by one, but they are all locked. Then I move on to the bathroom. The first bathroom window I try opens. It's a tight fit, but I am able to squeeze through. Once I'm in, I quietly slip into Lydia's room.

She's asleep on her bed, on top of the covers. She still has her robe on. I remember enough of life at this estate to realize that this is not right.

I touch her arm and whisper her name, trying to wake her. She doesn't move. I panic for a moment thinking that she is dead, but I can see her chest rise and fall shallowly.

It's then that I notice a fine dusting of powder on her collar, and I growl. They must have drugged her again. There will be no waking her until it wears off.

I inspect the cuff and chain. I'm hoping that I will be able to break it, but it's sturdy and strong.

When that fails, I study the lock on the cuff and try to commit it to memory so that I can explain it to Nanni. Maybe she will know where we can find the key.

Once I'm done, I spend a moment just studying her. She's so beautiful that it makes my heart swell. Once I get her free of this place, I will give her my mating bite so that she can stay with me always.

No one has hurt her, and I count that as a blessing. I long to stay with her so that she doesn't have to suffer this alone, but I know I can't.

Before I leave, I bend down and kiss the top of her head. I ache to kiss her lips, but I'm worried about that powder.

After I kiss her, I break a couple of mushrooms off my shoulder and tuck them into her hand. I hope that she will recognize them, and it will reassure her that I am here with her. I may not be at her side, but I can be with her from a distance.

I slip out of the bathroom window, then make my way back to Nanni's rooms.

Chapter 26

I GROAN AS I start to wake up. I must be coming down with something because I feel awful. Wait, I don't remember getting into bed. I scowl as I remember the powder that the servant blew into my face. Did they seriously drug me again?

I move my legs and feel something heavy around my ankle. I also hear the clink of metal. What?

I try to sit up but am hit with a wave of nausea that knocks me back down. I roll over and lean my head off the side of the bed and vomit all over the floor.

Yep, it's definitely that drug from before. I don't even feel bad for vomiting all over the place. It serves them right for doing that to me.

Once the nausea subsides, I realize that I'm holding something clenched in my fist. When I open my fist to look, I find two small, slightly crushed mushrooms. It takes me a moment to recognize them as the mushrooms that grow on Wold's shoulder. Wold! Hope explodes in my chest. He must be here! But where?

I shift on the bed again and hear the clink of metal and feel something tugging against my ankle. I look down to see a chain attached to an ankle cuff. What the...they chained me to the bed?!

The door opens and the two Elven servants come in, and I quickly slip Wold's mushrooms into my robe. One of the servants says good morning to me. I just glare at them.

One of them, the one that drugged me last night, starts to come around the side of the bed and gasps when she sees the vomit. She gives me a wide-eyed look. "What happened?"

I glare at her and coldly say, "You drugged me."

She puts her hands to her mouth. "But it shouldn't have made you sick."

The other servant comes around the bed to see what the fuss is about and grimaces when she sees it.

I say, "In case you forgot, I'm human. That's what it does to me. It also makes me feel like crap. Everything hurts and my head feels like it's going to split in two. So thanks for that. Also you CHAINED ME TO THE BED!"

I thought yelling would make me feel better, but it just hurts my head. I clutch my temples with both hands.

The servant genuinely looks dismayed. "I'm so sorry, it was our Lord's orders...I...I had to." She seems to catch herself though, then she straightens up and says, "How does a nice warm bath sound? I will draw you a bath and use the soaps with a calming scent."

I gag a little at the thought of anything scented, and it startles both of them. "Do you have any soaps without scents? That will probably be better."

She gives me a wide-eyed look and says, "Yes, I will go get them." Then she leaves the room.

She comes back a few minutes later with a small bundle in her hands, and immediately goes into the bathroom. I hear the water start running.

The other servant comes over to the foot of the bed and unlocks the cuff with a key from her pocket. Then she says, "Let's go to the bathroom so you can relieve yourself."

By the time I get into the bathroom, the tub is full of unscented bubbles. I have to admit, it looks wonderful. I can just imagine how soothing it will be to soak in it.

I ask them for privacy while I pee and get undressed. I also grab one of my hidden mushrooms and manage to choke it down. Then I hide the mushrooms Wold left me along with the other mushrooms.

I sigh as I slip into the tub and then I call out to the servants to let them know they can come back in.

They return and help me bathe.

It only takes me a few minutes to realize that the bath was a terrible mistake. I end up getting too hot very quickly, and that triggers my nausea again. We try to hurry to get me out of the bath quickly, but it wasn't fast enough, and I end up vomiting on the floor next to the tub.

The servants manage to get me dried off and into a nightgown, then they put me back in bed with a chamber pot so I have somewhere to throw up if I need to. After that, they get to work cleaning up the vomit. I drift off to sleep to the sounds of them working.

I'm awoken a little while later by one of the servants. She hands me bread and a glass of water. I sit up and take a fews sips of water first. Once I get those down, I ask, "What time is it?"

She replies, "Mid-afternoon."

"Mid-afternoon?" I say, completely surprised by how long I've slept.

"Yes, mid-afternoon. You were very sick this morning, so we thought it was best to let you sleep. Are you feeling any better?"

I think about it, and my head isn't hurting as badly and I'm not as nauseous. "I think I'm starting to feel better."

"I'm glad. We told Lord Varik that you weren't well, and that you likely would not be able to join him for dinner."

I watch her for a minute as she straightens some items on a shelf. Finally I say, "You can do that?"

She gives me a slightly confused look, then says, "Do what?"

"You can just tell him that I won't come to dinner because I don't feel well? Won't he be angry?"

"Oh, well in this circumstance we were able to. He would not want you vomiting in front of him," she says.

Of course it's just about him. He would hate for me to ruin his night with my disgusting vomiting. As much as I hate throwing up, I think it would be hilarious to vomit on him. Maybe I should try to convince her to let me go to dinner so I can have the chance. I try to sit up to set down my cup of water, and my head starts pounding again.

Ugh...maybe not. I lay back down still holding my cup.

The servant comes over and takes the glass from me, then puts it on the bedside table. She quietly says, "Rest today. Your Guardian's scent will be worn off of you by tomorrow. You will need your strength to deal with Lord Varik tomorrow night." She gives me a sad, knowing look.

Oh gods. Tomorrow.

Chapter 27

NANNI GOES TO THE house in the morning to see what she can find out about Lydia. She is friendly with one of the servants that takes care of Lydia. She gives me strict instructions to stay in her rooms. Before she leaves, she whispers to me that this would be a good time for me to get to know Pampa.

After Nanni leaves, I look at Pampa. She gives me an expectant look, but I do not know what to say to her. So I just continue to pace the rooms.

Pampa finally looks at me and asks, "You are my brother?"

I stop pacing to look at her. "Yes, it appears so." I watch her for a minute, then I ask, "What do you know of our birth mother?"

"Not a lot. I was very little when she died. I do know she never had much love for me. She probably would have sent me away like she did to you if she had lived."

"She was not a kind mother. I have always seen Nanni as my real mother," I explain. "You are lucky to stay here with Nanni."

She looks at me with fear in her eyes. "Nanni says she doesn't know how long Lord Varik will let me stay. She's trying to convince him that I am useful. But he doesn't want me here."

I remember what it felt like when I was facing my birth mother sending me away. I remember how afraid I was. "You could come live on my territory with me and Lydia. Nanni can come too if she is tired of being here. I have plenty of space, and I could teach you how to tend to the territory."

Her face lights up. "Really...you mean it?"

"Yes. No one should be trapped here."

I catch Nanni's scent before she opens the door. She has a worried look on her face when she enters her rooms.

"What is wrong? Is Lydia okay?" I ask immediately.

"Lydia is okay. I spoke with Faylen. She's one of Lydia's elven servants. Lord Varik made her drug Lydia with the same powder they used when she was kidnapped. It made her very sick today. She has been unwell and vomiting for most of the day," Nanni says.

I growl at this. Nanni puts her hand on my arm to calm me before I can get too worked up.

"This works in our favor. Lord Varik will not want to be around a person that is ill, so she will not have to see him today. Faylen says that your scent is fading on her, and she believes that Lord Varik will want to visit her bedchamber tomorrow night."

"No."

"We will get her before then," Nanni says.

"But how? How will we get to her? They are keeping her shackled to her bed!" I practically yell.

Nanni gives me a warning look that tells me I need to calm down. "Faylen will help us. She believes the other servant, Osonia, will also help us. Lord Varik...he is cruel to them when he has no other bedmates available. He forces one of them into his bed," she explains.

I growl again and Nanni pats on my arm.

"Osonia and Faylen can help us get Lydia out," she repeats.

"But what about the guards? There are too many of them for me—"

"Osonia has a lover that is a guard," Nanni explains. "They want to officially mate, but Lord Varik will not allow it, and he continues to require Osonia to...serve him...in his bed. Not only is her lover angry, but the other guards are also angry at the obvious disregard he has for them. And Faylen is well loved and admired among the household staff. I can think of several male servants or guards that would fight for a chance to be in her bed, although I think she has a soft spot for the Guardian that is our cook. I have seen the fury in his eyes on the nights she must go to Lord Varik. She is softer than Osonia, and many of us—myself included—have seen Faylen sobbing after leaving Lord Varik's rooms. He uses his glamour on them, and he is not... kind...or gentle with them.

"Just like your mother, Lord Varik does not have any allies in his home." She pauses for a moment and looks between me and Pampa, before continuing, "And just like with your mother, everyone would look the other way at his demise. Your mother made herself a thorn in the other nobles' sides. All of them were glad to be done with her when she was killed. Lord Varik has proven to be even worse than she was..." She pauses again, and a dark look crosses her face. "Some of the things he does..." She shakes her head. "I do not believe any authorities would demand justice for his death."

Fear and rage boil inside of me. He's a monster, and my Lydia is trapped with him. "How do we do it?"

Nanni rests her hand on my shoulder. "I will get word out with the staff. Everyone will need to be ready to leave. Faylen and Osonia will need to have Lydia ready as well."

"When? Tonight?"

Nanni just nods.

"Nanni, you and Pampa should come with us and live on my territory. I have more than enough room for all of us to have a home."

I can see the tears in Nanni's eyes when she says, "I would love that."

Pampa and I rest for the remainder of the day while Nanni whispers plans to the other household staff.

Chapter 28

I SPEND THE NEXT few hours in bed. When I wake up again, it's growing dark outside. One of the servants comes into the room and offers me some water and more bread. She asks if I would like to try to eat anything else. I groan and shake my head.

"Are you certain? It would be good for you to keep up your strength," she explains. She looks more nervous and on edge than she normally does.

"No, I don't think I could keep it down."

"Ah, well okay. Let's get you up so you can relieve yourself. Then we will get you dressed." She puts her hand on my upper back to gently guide me out of bed.

Once I use the bathroom, I choke down another mushroom. I honestly can't even remember when I ate my last one, and I don't even know if I kept it down. Then I go out into my room where the servant is quickly laying out clothes for me.

What she's picked out is not very elegant. It's still a dress, but it's not very fancy. I would even call it plain.

"I thought I wasn't going to dinner with Lord Varik tonight. Did something change?" I ask. I'm completely confused as to why she's getting me dressed.

"Oh no, you aren't. This is just so you are properly dressed...just in case..." She trails off at the end and doesn't explain why. I watch her for a few minutes. She's acting really strange. This servant is usually nicer and a little more casual than the other one, but there's something about the way she is doing things that almost feels frantic. It feels like something is going on and I just don't know about it.

Maybe I can figure out what's happening if I ask her a few questions.

"I feel bad, no one ever told me your name," I say.

She seems a bit surprised and stops in the middle of what she's doing so she can look at me. "Oh, it's Faylen. Lord Varik rarely uses our names. He probably doesn't really even know them. I guess we didn't think to introduce ourselves." She's folding some clothing, and she looks so sad as she does it. She lowers her voice to just above a whisper and says, "Lydia...I am very sorry for how you have been treated. Please know that it wasn't what I wanted."

Seriously, what is going on? I finally look down at what she's doing. She's folding some clothing and stuffing it into some sort of a bag. Some of the clothing she wraps around a few trinkets before she tucks it into the bag.

"Faylen...are we going somewhere?"

She presses her lips together, so they form a line, then she looks towards the door. She reaches into the pocket of her apron, takes something out, and hands it to me. When I open my hand, it's a couple of Wold's mushrooms! I gasp.

She presses her finger over her lips to remind me to stay quiet. Then she says, "Let's get you dressed." I nod enthusiastically.

As she is helping me into the dress, she quietly whispers to me that he is coming for me tonight.

As soon as the dress is on, I rush into the bathroom and grab my stash of mushrooms. I hand one to Faylen. "He won't be able to glamour you if you eat this," I explain. She quickly eats it.

She goes back to folding clothes, and I anxiously pace the room. Every sound sets me on edge, and I look out all of the windows hoping for a glimpse of Wold.

After about an hour, we hear quick footsteps coming down the hall. The other servant slips into the room. She looks frazzled and worried, which is strange because she's the one that always seemed so stoic and put together. She rushes over to Faylen.

"I think something is wrong. I can't find Haemir anywhere. The other guards said that Lord Varik requested a meeting with him. They haven't seen him since. He must still be with Lord Varik," she says with desperation in her voice. I can see the tears welling up in her eyes.

Faylen hugs her and comforts her. As she's rubbing her hand up and down the other servant's back, she says to me, "Haemir is Osonia's lover. He's one of the guards here."

Osonia must be the other servant's name. I'm so ashamed that I hadn't asked them their names before. I was just so angry with everything and everyone. I didn't want to know them so I couldn't sympathize with them.

Osonia is openly weeping now. "Haemir is no one important to Lord Varik. There is no reason that he should have been called in for a meeting. What if Lord Varik has glamoured him?"

The horror of what these poor people deal with on a daily basis starts to sink in. I get out another one of the mushrooms and quietly hand it to Osonia. "He won't be able to glamour you if you eat this." Osonia quickly eats it and thanks me.

As she swallows and goes back to quietly weeping, we hear the loud stomp of men's boots coming down the hall. Oh no, that can't be good.

LYDIA

Chapter 29

THE THREE OF US huddle together as far away from the door as we can get.

Lord Varik flings the door open and immediately storms into my room with three guards behind him. The guard standing closest to Lord Varik looks like he has been beaten. His face is a swollen bloody mess, and it looks like he's missing an ear, but he still stands with Lord Varik.

Osonia lets out a choked sob when she sees him. "Oh gods, Haemir! What did he do to you?"

Haemir and the other guards just stare at us and continue to stand there with their swords drawn. Their eyes look blank and glazed over as if they aren't really seeing anything.

Osonia cries, "Haemir!" She still gets no response.

Lord Varik begins laughing at her and says, "Did you really think you would get away with this little plan?"

Osonia gasps and says, "My lord, what plan? There is no plan."

Lord Varik laughs again. "Shut up, female. I know everything that happens here. I know of the plan to free *her*." He points to me as he says this.

He then directs his attention to me. "And *you*...you have quickly become more trouble than you are worth. You were supposed to just be a little bit of fun, someone new and interesting to fuck. I've never had a human woman before. I wanted to see what all the fuss is about."

He looks to Haemir. "Guards, seize them. I'm sure I can find a fun way to put them to good use."

When he says this, Faylen gasps and Osonia cries, "No!"

I push both of them behind me and glare at Lord Varik as I say, "What is wrong with you?! Stop this!"

He just laughs at me.

The guards come over and roughly grab each of us by the arm. They pull our hands behind us to bind them. As the guard holds my hands together, I begin to feel something cool and not quite liquid but also not quite solid slither its way around my wrists and over my hands, binding them tightly together.

I panic at the strange sensation and begin trying to yank my hands apart, but they are held tight. Now whatever it is that encases my hands feels solid and strong, like metal. I thrash and continue to yank, and then I notice that Lord Varik is laughing.

"Poor foolish girl. You truly are lost in a world that you don't understand, aren't you?"

I glare at him.

He smugly grins. "You didn't really think that I was without magic, did you? I know you knew about my glamour because you found some way to protect yourself against it. But that's all you thought I could do, isn't it?" He's laughing at me like there is some funny joke that I'm not a part of.

I don't find any of this funny at all, so I yell at him. "What are you talking about?"

Faylen quietly whispers, "Lydia..." I turn to look at her. She gives me a sad look and then looks down. I follow her gaze and gasp at what I see.

Liquid gold is covering her feet and slowly creeping up her calves. I look over at Osonia, and the same thing is happening to her. Both of them have tears running down their cheeks as they watch the gold's progression.

Horrified, I look to Lord Varik. He arches an eyebrow and smiles at me.

"You are doing this? You have to stop. You can't just cover them in gold, they'll die!"

He laughs again. "Oh...I can't? And what do I care if a servant dies?"

The realization hits me, and it feels like it knocks all the air out of me. "The statues...all of the golden statues...oh gods...they were people, weren't they?" I feel like vomiting. How many statues did I see around the estate? How many people has he killed?

He smiles at me, and says, "You see, some of my bedroom activities leave people...well...let's say, worse for the wear. I can't have injured lovers warning others away from my bed."

My stomach drops, and my pulse starts pounding in my ears. This is a sex thing? What kind of depravity leads to something like this? Gods, all those people! What must they have gone through? Bile burns at the back of my throat, and I feel like I'm going to vomit. I take a few deep breaths and manage to hold it back.

I desperately look around the room for some way out of this, but it's just us and the glamoured guards and Lord Varik. Once I see that there is nothing we can do, I begin to panic.

"Don't do this. Please let us go." I am begging, but I don't care at this point. "We will just disappear. Please...no one will ever know this happened."

He gives me a dark smile. "I know. You *will* just disappear." He gestures to Faylen and Osonia. "They already are. But I think I want to play with you a little bit first."

My blood runs cold with fear, and I have the overwhelming urge to run. Lord Varik must be able to sense it because the guard behind me clamps his strong hands around my upper arms and holds me in place.

Lord Varik calmly starts walking toward me. He stops at the side of the bed and carefully removes his shirt, then folds it and lays it on bed. His chest is a shimmering gold, which would be beautiful if it didn't house such a monstrous heart.

There's a large knife strapped to his belt, and he removes that too. He sets it on the bed next to his shirt. Then he removes his boots, and next his pants.

He straightens back up and I see that his cock is already hard and dripping pre-cum.

Oh no no no no.

This can't be happening.

Then he picks the knife back up.

I hear a little whimper of fear from Faylen.

Lord Varik's look turns dark, and he glares at Faylen. "Shut up, you disgusting whore. You've always been too weak."

He walks to her, and then lightly runs the tip of the knife down the side of her throat and then down her breastbone and stops in between her breasts. He's pressing it just hard enough draw a small drop of blood. Faylen is visibly trembling, she is so afraid. "I should have gotten rid of you ages ago. You never were any fun."

Suddenly I hear myself say, "Leave her alone."

He turns his dark gaze on me. "Would you rather I pay attention to you then?" And he walks over to me.

He's standing so close, that I can feel his cock brush up against me. I put on my bravest face and say, "Leave us alone."

He laughs smugly, then mockingly says, "I should leave you alone, should I?" His eyes are dancing with amusement at himself. Then he grabs a handful of my hair. He snarls in my face, "I think not."

I screech as he begins dragging me toward the bed by my hair. He roughly shoves me face first into the mattress so that I am bent over the side of the bed. I scream as he presses his body hard against me. While still gripping a handful of my hair, he reaches around with the other hand and holds the knife to my throat. I go completely still as terror fills me. I can feel the hard length of his cock pressed against my backside as he says, "I think I should get to enjoy my new toy at least once." He lets go of my hair, and I let out a sob as he fumbles with my skirts with one hand.

Just then I hear a feral roar coming from outside the window beside the bed. Something explodes through the window, and I scream as shards of glass shower down onto me.

I look up and Wold is crouched just beyond the foot of the bed, snarling at Lord Varik.

Chapter 30

I FILL WITH HOPE the moment I see Wold.

He snarls at Lord Varik as he crouches before us.

Lord Varik shifts to stand up, but is still pressed against me as he laughs and looks at Wold. "You must be Mother's first monster. No wonder she got rid of you. I never understood her fascination with Guardians. You are just disgusting beasts."

Wold just snarls again at him.

Lord Varik dismissively waves a hand at Wold and says, "Guards, kill him."

Osonia screams, "No!" But Haemir raises his sword and runs at Wold. Wold throws him against the wall and Haemir crumples to the floor, unconscious. Osonia sobs quietly behind me.

The other guards run at Wold, but he leaps through the air and slams another one into the wall. His hair vines whip out, wrap around the neck of the other guard, and fling him aside as well.

I watch in horror as Lord Varik begins melting and moving gold along the walls and floor to trap Wold. I suddenly realize that this whole estate is a giant weapon for Lord Varik. It's all covered in gold. Wold must realize it too because he moves faster as he leaps from wall to wall, using his claws just like he does in the trees. Wold is fast, but I notice as he leaps that one of his feet is starting to turn gold. Lord Varik must have gotten him, but it doesn't seem to slow Wold down.

Wold makes a final leap towards us, and grabs Lord Varik by the throat as he lands. He yanks Lord Varik away from me, and I roll off the bed. Lord Varik screams as Wold slams him against the closet door. Then his scream is broken off when Wold squeezes his throat and digs his claws in. Blood runs in little trails down Lord Varik's chest from his throat. Lord Varik tries to raise the knife against Wold, but Wold swats it out of his hand. Gold is beginning to climb up Wolds legs and tail. His feet are already covered in it, and it's working its way up to his knees.

Wold snarls in Lord Varik's face and says, "I think it is time for our mother's house to die." He squeezes Lord

Varik's throat tighter, digging his claws in deeper. Lord Varik's eyes are wide and budging as he tries desperately to gasp for air. He grabs Wold's arm trying to break his grip, but he isn't strong enough. He does manage to leave behind a handprint-sized smudge of gold on Wold's arm. Then Wold stabs the claws of his other hand into Lord Varik's lower stomach and slices them up to his ribcage, eviscerating him. Blood pours from the wounds as Lord Varik's organs begin sliding out of the slices. Wold lets go of Lord Varik's throat, and blood begins pouring out as Wold's claws slide out of the wounds they made. Lord Varik crumples to the floor and makes a little gurgling noise before he finally goes still.

Everything is quiet for just a moment, then I begin to see the gold melt off of Wold's legs and arm. I feel it melting off of my hands too. I look at Osonia and Faylen. It's melting off of their hands and feet as well. But something is different. I can see the gold running off of them, but their skin looks like it's stained gold. I look at my own hands, and even though they are no longer bound, they are stained gold and feel tingly and numb.

Osonia pushes past me and stumbles to Haemir's side. She says his name over and over again as she tries to wake him. After a few moments, he groans and opens his eyes. When he sees Osonia, he croaks out her name. "I couldn't fight it. I'm so sorry, Osonia." She bursts into tears again, and buries herself in his chest.

I gasp and realize that I've been holding my breath. Then I run to Wold and fling myself into his arms. Blood smears all over my arms and dress, but I don't care. I begin sobbing as he holds me.

A loud commotion comes behind us. In the doorway stands a massive Guardian wearing an apron and wielding a huge, long-handled meat cleaver as if he's ready to go to battle. He must be the cook. He's covered in mostly white fur with dark leopard-like spots. His features are mostly cat-like, and he has a long fluffy tail. But he also has tall, proud horns that stick straight up from his head and curve only slightly towards the back.

He's breathing heavily as he surveys the room, then his eyes lock on Faylen. "Faylen, are you well?" She has tears streaming down her face, and I see her shake her head before a half dozen guards run up behind the cook. All of them are Elven, and are all different gemstone shades.

The cook strides into the room and straight toward Faylen. He picks her up and carries her out of the room like he's carrying his bride.

A couple of the guards rush to Osonia's side. They help Haemir stand and support him between them as they begin walking from the room. One of them looks at Osonia and says, "Come. His things are packed and are waiting with your bags. We need to get out of here." Osonia follows them as they leave the room.

The remaining guards pick up the other two that Wold knocked unconscious and carry them out. I'm assuming they are going to get their things and leave too.

Wold looks at me and strokes his bloody hand down my cheek. "We need to go too. Nanni and Pampa are waiting for us in the servant quarters."

I sniffle a little and say, "Nanni and Pampa? Nanni is here?"

Wold smiles and carries me toward the door. He steps over Lord Varik's blood-soaked body and walks out the door and into the corridor. "I'll explain everything when we get to the servant quarters."

Chapter 31

I CARRY LYDIA THROUGH the corridors toward the tunnel that leads to the servant quarters. All along the corridor, where there used to be gilded golden details on the walls and ceiling, there is now flaking, crumbling, and melting gold. There were previously golden statues lining the hallway, and now there are old bodies lying on the floor in puddles of crumbling, melted gold. Lydia gasps when she sees them.

"He...he turned people into gold statues. He encased them in gold to kill them and now that all of that gold is melting off of them. Oh gods, they look mummified. These poor people." She buries her face against my chest and starts to cry.

The door leading to the tunnel is propped open when we get there. I assume it's because all the other servants went this way to leave.

We quietly walk down the tunnel and immediately go to Nanni's room.

When we walk in, Nanni and Pampa are anxiously waiting for us. There are a few bags packed and waiting by the door. Pampa jumps up and runs toward us as soon as we walk into the room. She stops short when she gets a good look at all the blood covering me. She gives me a wide-eyed look but doesn't ask about it. Nanni walks over to us and asks "Is that Lord Varik's blood? Is he dead?"

"Yes."

Nanni nods her head. "Good." Then she smiles at Lydia and says, "You must be Lydia. It is very nice to finally meet you." She turns towards Pampa. "This is Pampa. She's Wold's sister. I've been raising her here at this estate the same way that I raised Wold."

Lydia practically jumps out of my arms and exclaims, "Nanni! I'm so happy to finally meet you. Wold has told me a lot about you." Lydia starts to raise her arms like she is going to hug Nanni but then remembers all the blood. She looks down, a little embarrassed. "I'll save hugs for later."

Nanni gives Lydia a huge smile. "I feel like I should clarify that Nanni was just the nickname that Wold gave me because he couldn't say my real name, which is Nan-nitem."

Lydia hugs my waist and says, "That's adorable!"

I don't remember any of that, and I'm suddenly embarrassed by it. I just smile at them and scratch my neck awkwardly.

Nanni sees my discomfort and gives me a sweet smile. "It's a nickname that I love though. I've asked everyone to call me Nanni since Wold first started calling me that."

Lydia turns to Pampa and gives her a huge smile. "It's so nice to meet you too! You are so beautiful...and you look just like Wold! I'm so excited that he has family."

Pampa gives her a shy smile. "You are just as pretty as the servants said you are."

Lydia thanks her and says, "I'll give you a big hug just as soon as I'm not all bloody anymore."

Nanni interjects, "Then let's get you two cleaned up. We need to leave soon and not have you two covered in blood." She rummages around for something to help us clean off

Pampa looks excitedly at Lydia. "Wold said we can come live with you and him!"

Lydia gives me a quick uncertain glance, then she says, "Oh that would be perfect!"

Nanni hands me one of Lord Varik's plush towels, and I begin scrubbing all the blood off me. Then she brings

Lydia a dress and says, "I asked Faylen to give me a spare dress for you. I had a feeling you might end up with ruined, bloody clothes."

Nanni wipes the blood off Lydia's face, arms, and chest, then helps her change into the new dress. As soon as the dress is on and laced up, Lydia spins around and startles Nanni with a huge hug. She releases her, and sweeps Pampa up in a hug as well.

We gather the bags that Nanni and Pampa packed and immediately leave to start our journey back to my territory. It will be a long walk, and I am concerned about Lydia being able to walk the distance.

Nanni pauses. "Let's see if there is a cart and horse. Lydia has had a difficult time over the past couple of days; it might be a lot for her to walk all the way there."

As we walk toward the stables, a female voice calls out to Nanni. When I turn, I see that it came from one of the females that had been in Lydia's room.

Nanni rushes toward the female. "Faylen! I'm so glad that you are safe. Are you leaving?"

Faylen gives her a shy look and blushes a slightly deeper orange. Then she says, "Yes, I'm leaving with Allium."

She turns to look over her shoulder. There I see the cat-like Guardian cook watching us. He is holding the reigns of a horse and has a large pack on his back. His scent is all over the small female.

Nanni gives her a knowing smile and says, "I'm glad that you two finally got together."

Faylen smiles back at Nanni. "Me too. We are going to the nearest town to look for work. We even mentioned opening an inn for travelers."

"That's a wonderful idea. I'm so glad I got to say good-bye to you. Good luck on your new adventure." Nanni gives Faylen a tight hug, and I can see the tears starting to slide down her cheeks.

Faylen then comes over to Lydia. All my muscles tighten at the thought of a threat to Lydia, but she just looks at Lydia and says, "I'm so sorry for everything that happened. It was never any of my idea. I think we could have been great friends if we'd met under different circumstances. Thank you for helping to free us from...*him*."

Lydia gives her a hug and says, "I understand completely. Maybe one day Wold and I can come visit you."

After their embrace, Faylen walks back to the cook. He helps her up onto the horse, then climbs on behind her. He nods to me as they ride away.

***

Once we are inside the stable, I am relieved to find that there are still two carts and several horses left.

Nanni says, "Pampa and I will hitch one of the horses up to the cart." They head toward a white mare. The horse doesn't seem nervous around them, so I assume that Lord Varik made them do this a lot. Lydia wanders over to them and pets the horse, then watches as they hitch her to the cart.

Once they are done, we walk the horse out of the stable. Nanni and Pampa ride up front to guide the horse, while Lydia and I lay down in the back.

Pampa turns around and excitedly says, "Nanni says she will show me how to drive the horse! Don't worry, Wold and Lydia, I will drive us to our new home!"

Nanni laughs and shakes her head. "Pampa, turn around and pay attention. They have had a long night; let them rest."

As soon as we get moving, Lydia curls up against me with her head on my chest. She whispers, "Thank you for saving me, Wold."

As I curl up with her, I whisper back, "I will always come for you, my little sprite." Before I know it, we have both fallen asleep.

Chapter 32

I END UP SLEEPING in the back of the cart for most of the night with my head on Wold's chest while he holds me. When I wake up, the sun is starting to rise. I notice someone else curled up next to me, and I look to see that it's Pampa. She must have gotten tired in the night and curled up in the back to sleep. I pet her hair, but don't wake her. Just seeing her there brings a smile to my face.

I look up at Wold and see the glow of his eyes, he is already awake. He smiles at me and strokes my hair.

I whisper, "How long do we have before we are back on your territory?"

"Not that long. We are almost to the town where the market is held. We are going to sell the horse and cart there, and we will have to walk the rest of the way like we did when we went to the market."

"That's good. I can't wait to be back." Then I hesitantly say, "Wold, when do I have to go back to my world?"

Wold cups my cheek with his palm and with a smile says, "Never."

I gasp, then remember that Pampa is still sleeping, so I excitedly whisper, "Never?! I can stay? But what about safety?"

"When Guardians take a mate, they give their mate a mating bite. I only knew a little about it, but I knew enough that I knew I couldn't give you my bite if I wanted you to be able to go home. So I was careful not to bite you. When I found Nanni at Lord Varik's estate, she explained that the mating bite would have kept you safe, and no one would have tried to kidnap you. If I had only known..." Wold trails off at that and looks devastated.

I reach up and kiss him, "Hey, it's not your fault. You didn't know that about mating bites, you didn't have anyone to teach you about that. You got me back, and I'm fine. You also found Nanni and Pampa! Don't blame yourself for me getting kidnapped."

He smiles at me and hugs me closer. "When we get back to my territory, I can give you my mating bite and we will be bound together...if that is still what you want."

I can't help myself. I squeal. I clap my hand over my mouth when I remember that I am supposed to be quiet because Pampa is asleep. She stirs a little, and rolls to her other side, but fortunately she doesn't wake up.

"Of course I still want to stay with you, silly!" I whisper. "I want to spend all of my days with you." Then I slide on top of him so I can give him a kiss. He kisses me back fiercely, and I can feel his fear and uncertainty melting away with that kiss. He slips his long tongue into my mouth, tangling it with mine, and I lose myself in that kiss.

After a minute, I hear a small giggle in the back of the cart with us. Pampa. We stop kissing, and I look up and Pampa is awake and smiling at us. I smile back at her and tell her good morning.

Pampa hops up next to Nanni and scoots to sit right at her side. Wold sits up and checks on Nanni. "Are you doing okay? Do you need to come back here and rest?"

Nanni looks tired, but she smiles and says, "No, the town is just ahead. I would rather get to your cave and rest there."

It only takes us about ten or fifteen more minutes before we are at the small town. Without the market, there isn't much left to see. There is an inn with a tavern downstairs, and attached to the inn is a general store-type shop.

Nanni and Pampa go into the tavern to speak with the owners about selling the horse and cart, while Wold and I stay with the cart. I take the opportunity to hug Wold around the waist and snuggle against him.

Nanni and Pampa come back out of the inn a short time later. They are followed by a Guardian that looks very similar to the cook that rescued Faylen. He mostly inspects the horse, but he also looks over the cart, then he says to Nanni, "We have a deal." He heads back into the inn and brings a bag of coins to Nanni, then he leads the horse and cart around to the back of the inn.

I glance over at Wold, and he is looking thoughtfully at the shop. He turns to Nanni, "Did we get a fair price for the horse and cart?"

"Fair enough."

"Then we should see if we need anything else," he says, and he leads us into the shop.

They have a little bit of everything in the shop. There are some simple clothes like dresses and tunics and trousers. Wold takes me over to those first and we pick out a few things so that I have a couple of sets of clothes.

Wold then finds some bars of soap, and hands a couple of them to me. Without thinking about it, I hold them each up to my nose to see what the scent is. It probably shouldn't surprise me that they are unscented since everyone here is sensitive to smells. Wold gives me a curious look when I do this.

"Sorry, it's habit. In our world, soaps are scented so that you smell nice when you get done showering."

"I'm glad we aren't in your world; I only want to smell you." I smile at him for saying that.

Pampa and Nanni were exploring other parts of the shop, and we walk back towards them. They are each carrying a few things. I look at what Nanni is holding, and it looks like practical tools and utensils for cooking, and Pampa seems to be helping by carrying a few more items like that.

Wold pauses to look at a wall of tools. He grabs an axe and tests its weight and sharpness. Then he picks up a small hand saw.

"What are those for?" I ask.

He looks a little embarrassed. "I don't want you to have to live in a cave. I thought I could work on building a home for you."

I gasp and then I drop the items that I was holding and fling myself against him. He almost drops the axe that he was holding, but he sets it down against the wall and wraps his arms around me too.

I have tears in my eyes when I say, "I would love for us to build a home together."

He strokes his claws through my hair and just holds me for a minute. I finally look back up at him. "Thank you for coming to save me."

"They never could have kept you from me. I would have torn apart both of our worlds to get to you if I had to." Then he kisses me. We kiss for a moment before I hear Pampa giggling again, and I break the kiss to look at her. I just smile and shake my head.

Then I get an idea. I look back at Wold, and say, "I think we embarrass Pampa with our kissing. Obviously, that means we will just have to do it more." I reach up and pull his face back down to mine for more kissing, and I hear a little squeal from Pampa and a lot more giggling.

Nanni laughs and finally says, "Do we have everything we need? I'm eager to get back to Wold's cave and rest."

I remember that Nanni hasn't slept, and it sobers me. "Yes, I think we are ready, right Wold?"

I look up at Wold and see him looking at a few stuffed toys in a basket. He walks over to the basket and picks one up. It's a fabric doll made to look like a Guardian. It's bark-colored and has yarn and fabric vines for hair. The legs, feet, and tail look cat-like, just like Wold and Pampa.

Pampa watches him with huge eyes. Then he hands the doll to her. "Here, you should have the things children have."

She hugs the doll to her chest and says, "Thank you, Wold." I see tears in her eyes, and I wonder if anyone has ever given her a toy before. Poor Pampa, and poor Wold. The two of them have had their childhoods stolen from them, and the thought of that crushes me.

I'm still thinking about this after we pay the shopkeeper and leave. Wold must notice that something is wrong, and he pulls me to the side and asks if I'm alright.

"When you gave Pampa the doll, I realized that the two of you have basically had your childhoods stolen from you. You were never allowed to be real children. And that makes me so sad."

Wold strokes my hair and then says, "Pampa's childhood isn't gone yet. She still has time. Hopefully we can help her have that." This makes me smile and feel a bit better.

Pampa is still young. We still have time to turn things around for her.

Chapter 33

WE MAKE GOOD TIME walking back home. The edge of my territory isn't very far from the market grounds, so it doesn't take us very long to reach it. As we near my territory, Lydia points to a tree ahead of us.

"That's where your territory begins, right? I remember that tree," she says. I notice Pampa perk up and look at it.

I nod. I can feel the borders of my territory, so I don't need landmarks to note where it is, but I'm glad that she noticed this one.

We continue walking and cross into my territory. I feel it the moment I am on my land. I can't describe it, but it just feels like I'm home. I let the land's magic run through me, and I don't feel that there is anything wrong in my territory. I sense no intruders.

I notice that Pampa has a curious look on her face. She's clinging to her doll, and I can tell she is thinking deeply about something. I ask, "Pampa, is something wrong?"

She gives me a surprised look and says, "No, I just...it feels strange. It feels like home."

I smile at her because I understand exactly what she means.

Nanni says, "It is because you two are siblings. This is your territory too, Pampa. Wold is the oldest, so he is bound to it, but you will still feel the lands magic because it also belongs to you."

Pampa smiles, hugs her doll tightly, and whispers to herself. "It's mine too."

***

As we make our way back toward the mushroom cave, Lydia tells Pampa about all the things I've shown her here. About the little burrow I slept in underneath the tree, and all the bioluminescent mushrooms that I took there so I wouldn't be afraid of the dark. About the mushroom cave itself. About the cliff, and even about how I plant some of the mushrooms from my cave around my territory. The way that she describes everything, I can tell how much she really loves it here. I've never imagined that I could find someone that loved my little slice of this world as much as I do. I want to make this a home for her.

I am lost in thought, planning the things I would need to make this a home for Lydia as I walk, so I do not notice the passing of time. Before I know it, I can see the entrance to the cave up ahead. I point it out to Pampa, and she lets out a little squeal and dashes up ahead.

When we reach the cave, she is peaking around the entrance trying to get a look inside. Lydia laughs. "Follow me, Pampa, I will show you around."

I set down the tools I purchased, and look around at the outside of the cave where Lydia and I built a fire and ate the rabbits I caught. She has been here for such a short amount of time, and already she is making a huge mark on this place.

Nanni comes up beside me. "It is nice to be back here. I missed this place. I wanted to stay with you so badly, but your mother would never allow it. I dreamed about being here, though." She sighs and looks around. "We will have much to teach Pampa."

I say, "Yes, I guess her first lesson will come today when we hunt rabbits."

Nanni smiles. "I remember how excited you were when you got your first rabbit."

From outside, we can hear Lydia and Pampa excitedly chattering.

We go in just in time to hear a splash as Pampa jumps into the pool of water. Lydia is watching her and laughing. I notice that Lydia is holding Pampa's doll for her. When we walk up, she says, "Sorry, Wold, I hope you don't mind...I told her that she could go swimming."

Nanni says, "I think a swim sounds lovely." Then she takes off both of the fabric pieces that she has wrapped around herself and wades out into the water too. Pampa happily splashes Nanni as soon as she gets the chance.

Lydia is standing at the edge of the water and laughing at them. I walk over to her and stroke her hair. "Are you going to swim?"

She says, "I don't have anything to wear in the water."

I'm confused, so I say, "You are not shy about being naked."

She smirks. "Not around you...that's different. Where I'm from, humans don't really get naked around each other to bathe. We do it in private, or we have clothes for swimming that we wear."

"But you took all of your clothes off to swim the day you met me."

She sighs. "That was different. I thought you wouldn't be back for a long time, so I thought I had time. Also...I thought you were hot, so I didn't mind if you came back and caught me naked."

I'm confused again. "What does 'hot' mean?"

She giggles. "Attractive. I liked you. I was attracted to you. That's what that means."

I smile and hug her to me, wrapping my tail around her leg. She lays her head against my chest and hugs me back. We stay embraced like this for several minutes, just enjoying holding each other again. Then I hear Nanni say, "Pampa, I think Lydia and Wold need some time to themselves, we can see them again tomorrow. Let's see if we can find the tree with the burrow under it that Wold was using as a place to sleep. It will be good scenting practice for you, and I think that would be a good place for you and me to sleep tonight. After we find it, I can teach you how to hunt for rabbits."

Pampa giggles when Nanni says that Lydia and I need time alone, but she perks up at Nanni's mention of hunting rabbits. "You will teach me to hunt? Really?!" Then she darts out of the water and bounces around doing her best to shake the water off, flinging water on us in the process.

As Lydia hands Pampa her doll back, she laughs and says, "I think we need to get some towels."

Nanni comes walking out of the water and uses the fabric she was wearing to dry off as much as she can. She then lays it out to dry. She stands back up and turns to Pampa. "Okay, we can go."

Pampa gives her a wide-eyed surprised look, then says, "Nanni, you aren't going to wear anything?"

Nanni laughs and says, "I only wore those because I spent so much time around the Elven. Guardians do not worry about such things."

Pampa gives her a huge grin. "We don't have to act proper here?"

Nanni smiles back. "Of course not. We can be ourselves here."

Nanni follows as Pampa scurries out of the cave.

Chapter 34

I SMILE AS I watch Nanni and Pampa leave. Pampa is so cute, she's so excited. I look up at Wold, and he is watching them leave too. I say, "I'm glad we found them and that they could come back with us."

"I'm glad we could save Pampa from what I went through."

I hug him a little tighter and bury my face against his chest, just trying to breathe in his scent. All of my emotions about everything that we have been through in these last few days crash over me, and I start to cry. Wold notices and begins stroking my hair and just holds me.

Finally, he says, "You are safe Lydia, it is okay now. I will never let anything like that happen again."

I sniff and wipe at my eyes. "I never really believed how dangerous it was. I just kind of thought you were being paranoid. But it happened! You were right the whole time. And we tried to be careful...we were so careful..." By this point I'm crying too much to continue. He hugs me tighter as I sob.

With my face practically buried in his chest I choke out, "It was so terrible, Wold."

He just holds me and strokes my hair to comfort me as I cry. Eventually he says, "My mating bite will keep you safe. You do not need to worry, my little sprite."

He tilts my face up and wipes my tears off with a knuckle. Then he leans in and kisses me. I kiss him back, and I feel the brush of his tongue against my lips. I open for him and his tongue immediately presses into my mouth, claiming me. He devours me with that kiss, and I let him. I want to feel all of him. After everything that happened, I need to feel him. I can feel his desperation as he thrusts his tongue into my mouth. His tongue is so long that I'm almost overwhelmed by it, but I need it at the same time. His fangs graze my cheek as he begins kissing and licking his way down my neck.

I whisper, "Wold...the mating bite. Don't we need to—"

He cuts me off when he nips my neck with his fangs, and I gasp. His voice is almost a growl as he says, "We will. This first. I need to feel you, to know you are still here." Then he throws his arms around me and picks me up. I squeak in surprise, wrapping my legs around his waist as he carries me to our glowing mushroom room.

He skims his fingertips along the wall as we walk in, and all the mushrooms light up.

I gasp even though I expected it. "I will never get tired of seeing that."

He looks at me with his gaze full of longing. "Good."

He sets me on our boulder and begins tugging at different places on my dress, trying to figure out how to take it off.

I giggle and then say, "Here, I think loosening these will help." I sit up on my knees to loosen the laces running down the back, and then we slip it over my head.

Wold tosses it on the floor and then pulls me against him. He kisses and licks along my neck and then onto my shoulder. While kissing me, he climbs onto the boulder and gently presses me down onto my back.

He lays his body between my thighs and buries his face between my breasts. I feel his tail wrap around one of my thighs. My fingers tangle into his hair and vines, and I hear him take a deep breath in. Then I gasp as his licks from my chest all the way up the side of my neck.

He licks my neck again, then whispers, "Lydia, without you, I am lost."

I whisper back, "You will never lose me again."

He licks my neck one more time, then begins to slide down my body. He hooks my legs over his shoulders and then slides that long tongue over my pussy. I grab onto his antlers and moan as he continues to lick me. Each lick ratchets up the pleasure until I am gasping and moaning and completely lost in it. Then he teases my clit with the forked tip of his tongue, and I feel like I could come apart just from that. "Oh fuck, Wold!"

He must sense how close I was to coming because he stops for a moment to growl, "Not yet." I feel my pussy clamp just from that.

He goes back to licking me in long strokes, then he thrusts his tongue into me, filling me with it. He continues thrusting it into me, fucking me with his tongue. With each thrust, he goes a little further, until I can feel his fangs pressing against the insides of my thighs. I know he has opened his jaw impossibly wide again. I feel so full of his tongue; I moan as each thrust stretches me and pushes me closer and closer to coming. I know his tongue must be doubled over inside me, stretching me and fucking me. Just when I feel like his tongue can't possibly be any longer, he thrusts it into me one more time. I feel his second set of fangs press against my skin. Suddenly I feel eight little bright pinpricks of delicious pain as his fangs break through the skin. The pleasure and the pain twine together as one and I gasp and writhe in it. Every movement I make presses his fangs harder into my skin and presses his tongue further into me. I'm at the very edge of my orgasm and I manage to gasp out, "Wold...please..."

Holding onto his antlers, I moan as I grind against his mouth and I can feel the back of his tongue press against my clit, and gods it feels amazing. I grind harder, and I know his fangs must be sinking into my skin, but all I feel is hot pleasure. The next time I grind against him, he lets out a feral growl from deep in his throat. I feel the vibrations of that growl everywhere, and it pushes me over the edge. I scream as my orgasm tears through me and then keeps going. My pussy pulses around his tongue and he holds me firmly in place as my hips try to buck wildly against him. As I finally begin to come down from my orgasm, he slips his tongue out of me and gently licks my pussy and the places where his fangs pierced my skin.

With a raspy voice, he looks up at me. "Lydia, are you hurt?"

I gasp and say, "No...gods that was amazing." I grab his antlers and guide him up to me. When his face is level with mine, I say, "I need you to fuck me, Wold."

He groans and slicks his glowing cock through the folds of my pussy, then presses it to the entrance of my core. I gasp as he slowly sinks into me and begins to fuck me. Gods, I can feel every ridge of his cock as he thrusts into me. I'm clinging to him and moaning when I notice a warm tingling feeling on my scalp and ears. I have no idea what the feeling is; he must be fucking me so well that my head is tingling. I just ignore it and continue enjoying the feeling of his cock slowly dragging in and out of me.

He thrusts into me again and then pauses inside me. With a husky voice he says, "Lydia…" Then he touches something on my head. It's above my head but I can almost feel him touching me. It's strange, it tugs like it's attached to me.

"Lydia, feel this. You have antlers."

I gasp, "What?"

I reach my hands up and feel two small antlers. They feel like Wold's, but they are much smaller than his. "Oh my gods, what…"

Then he strokes a claw along my ear, but something is different about that too. It feels too long. I reach for my ears and find they now come to little elegant points.

I gasp again and look at Wold. "How?"

He smiles and says, "The mating bite." Then he buries his face in my neck and inhales deeply. "Your scent, it's yours, but it's also mine."

I look into his eyes, and they are glowing brighter than I've ever seen them. I say, "I'm yours now." His eyes flair even brighter.

His voice is almost a growl as he says, "Mine. No one can take you from me now." Then he grabs my hips and thrusts into me hard. I moan as he fucks me. I can tell he isn't holding back this time. He hasn't lost control; he just isn't worried anymore. He's claiming me. On his next thrust, I feel his tendril unwrap from around his cock. It slides through the folds of my pussy and brushes past my clit. It continues to move and brush my clit in different ways, and I cry out at how good it feels. I cling to him as every thrust pushes me closer and closer to the edge.

While he's fucking me, Wold leans down and licks up the side of my neck. Then he growls in my ear, "Come for me, my little sprite." That command is all I need, and I scream his name as I come.

That pushes him over the edge, and he roars as he comes inside me.

As he's coming down from his orgasm, he collapses on top of me. He begins kissing and licking along my neck and chest.

I let out a little contented sigh as he does this. I say, "I'm yours forever."

He buries his face into my neck and groans, then says, "Forever."

***

We lay tangled up in each other for a long time. We don't really speak, we just enjoy being together. My heart feels so full. I can feel that we are connected now.

I'm stroking my fingers through his hair when I realize that the gold staining on my hands and arms is mostly gone. I just have the barest hint of it left on my fingers.

"Wold, look...my hands..."

He looks at them and says, "It must have been the mating bite." He thinks about it for a minute and then says, "It never stained my skin or fur. Maybe it is something to do with Guardians, and now that you are mated to a Guardian, my magic is in you and healed you."

I spread my fingers and look at the staining, then I say, "Even though it came from something awful, I think it looks pretty like this."

Wold takes my hand and kisses my fingers. "I think it's pretty because it is a part of you."

Then we go back to quiet, contented, cuddling.

LYDIA

Epilogue

Five years later

I'm out in the garden picking vegetables with Nanni when I hear the high-pitched maniacal laughter of my son, followed by Pampa's disgruntled muttering.

Nanni says, "Roscoe must be giving Pampa trouble again today. You know how he loves to get her worked up."

I laugh, "I think everything gets her worked up these days."

Nanni smiles. "Don't let her hear you say that."

I just giggle at that. Pampa is just now becoming a teenager, and it turns out that fae teenagers aren't all that different than human teenagers. They have a lot of big feelings, and everything pushes their buttons.

I yell, "Roscoe!! You play nice with Pampa!"

We were so surprised when I found out that I was pregnant with Roscoe. None of us knew that Wold could get me pregnant since I had been human. The mating bite changed all of that, though.

I had no idea what to expect. I didn't know if I would have one baby, or a few. We also had no idea what the baby would look like. He ended up being just one baby, and he is the perfect blend of me and Wold. His skin is a slightly darker shade of brown than mine, and he has adorable green freckles like Wold. He has antler nubs, so he will have antlers when he's older. He also has one little leaf that sticks straight up on the top of his head. I think that means he will have at least one hair vine when he gets older.

Much to his dismay, he doesn't have Wold's long claws and tail. He says they would be good for climbing, and he hasn't given up hope on them "coming in" as he gets older. I secretly thank the Gods that he doesn't have those. I can't imagine dealing with him being able to climb like Wold, plus his little fingers and toes are green and they are so adorable.

I can see Roscoe's wild, wavy, green hair as he sprints up to the garden. I already know that he has been antagonizing Pampa because his eyes are glowing a bright yellow with excitement.

I'm glad to see that he is still wearing his shorts. Most of the time I am able to get them on him in the morning, only for them to disappear by the afternoon. It's been an ordeal getting him to wear clothes because he wants to "be free like Guardians". Unfortunately, he is built more like a human or an Elven and all of his boy parts are on the outside. We've had several conversations about why no one needs to see his junk except him, a healer, and his future mate.

As he runs into the garden, he springs right onto my back and holds on like he's a little monkey. He cackles, "I can't help it if I'm faster than she is."

She storms up, pouting. "You are NOT faster than me. You cheated, and that's how you won."

Roscoe growls through his small fangs. "Did not! The rules changed, that's all."

I sigh. "Come on, you two, help us harvest the vegetables. We are planning to trade some of them tonight at the market."

Both of their eyes light up; they both love going to the market. I can't blame them. It's such a magical place. We still have to be careful, but things have gotten a lot safer at the market, so we feel comfortable going as a family.

Faylen and Allium bought the tavern and inn that's in the small town where the market sets up. It turns out that the vendors must pay to use the land when they set up the market. Since the tavern is part of that land, whoever owns the tavern also owns the land.

Allium has taken it upon himself to clean up the market and make it safer for everyone. There used to be a travelling brothel that set up with the market, but apparently they were trafficking fae, so Allium doesn't allow them at the market any longer.

He also brought in several of his brothers to help with security. They patrol the market and kick out anyone that is up to no good.

We all love visiting the tavern and catching up with them. I love getting to see Faylen. She and Allium have a bunch of little ones of their own now. The oldest two are the same age as Roscoe. They are twin boys, and they all love rough housing together. They also have a set of triplets, two boys and one girl, who are about a year old now. They are the sweetest little babies you have ever seen, but I have no idea how Faylen manages with all those little ones. She is so happy now, and that's all that matters. I love seeing her happy.

Roscoe says, "When will Daddy be home?"

"When he's done harvesting the mushrooms for the market."

Roscoe sighs. He loves helping Wold, and he was very grumpy that he didn't get to help with the mushroom harvest today. He's going to be even more grumpy when I tell him that he's about to have to take a nap so that he's well rested for the market tonight.

We pick a few more vegetables and then I say, "Okay, I think that's enough. We have to leave enough green stuff for us."

I hear Roscoe pretend to retch. "Bleh."

"Hey...I heard that. Vegetables are good for you! You better start liking them because I'm going to trade some of these for seeds of even more vegetables."

Roscoe groans.

I begin to feel that little tug in my chest that always knows where Wold is. I can tell he's on his way home. "Come on, I think Daddy will be home soon. Let's go back to the house."

Wold built us a beautiful log cabin-style house. It connects to the mushroom cave, so Wold doesn't even have to leave to tend to his mushrooms. It also allows me and Wold to keep the bioluminescent mushroom room as our bedroom. I did convince him to bring a mattress in while I was pregnant with Roscoe. Sleeping on a boulder just wasn't cutting it anymore.

We built a large garden on the land that Wold cleared for lumber. We were able to trade at the market for seeds and roots to get it started.

We were even able to get some chicks, and now we have a little flock of colorful fae chickens. They drive Wold crazy because they like to sneak around and peck at his mushrooms. I catch him threatening to eat one of them at least once a day.

With the help of Allium, we were able to build a wood-burning oven outside beside the house. Nanni has fallen in love with cooking, and spends most of her days experimenting and making amazing dishes for us. She's gotten very good at it.

Nanni, Pampa, and Roscoe each have their own rooms in our house. Pampa still loves Wold's old burrow though. She frequently takes Roscoe "camping" there.

Wold has been talking about clearing some more trees for lumber to build a house around it for Pampa. She will eventually want a home of her own, and she loves the burrow so much. She has mentioned that sleeping there was the first time she felt like herself. She'd never felt like a Guardian at Lord Varik's home, and sleeping underground surrounded by glowing mushrooms really made her feel at peace and at home. She finally felt connected to her family's territory and felt what it was like to be a Guardian.

Wold still bears the burden of protecting his land from humans, but we have managed to get him to switch back to a daytime schedule. I know he's always afraid that a human will wander in and he will have to kill them.

I made "No Trespassing – Private Property" signs that we hung along the border, and they seemed to help a lot. We eventually built an old-fashioned log fence along the sections of the border that had the most problems with humans. Those seemed to have worked the best to deter people from wandering in. I can't even remember the last time Wold had to run off to scare away a human. Even when someone has ignored the fence and snuck in, a quick loud roar from Wold is usually enough to send them running back the way they came.

I can tell that it has lifted a weight off Wold. He seems to be at peace now.

As we are walking up to the house, I can see Wold standing in our outside "kitchen" area. He has a bag stuffed full of mushrooms from today's harvest.

Roscoe squeals when he sees Wold and takes off running straight to him. Once he's close, he flings himself at Wold, who easily catches him.

"Daddy! Did you harvest a lot of mushrooms? Momma says we are going to trade some of them for even *more* vegetables." With that, Roscoe makes a gagging face. "Why can't we just eat rabbit, Daddy? Oh, we could eat the chickens too!"

Wold just laughs and shakes his head. Nanni, Pampa, and I reach the house and set our baskets of vegetables down.

I immediately go to Wold and wrap my arms around him. I missed him even if he was only gone for a little bit. He balances Roscoe on one arm and wraps the other one around me, then he bends down and gives me a kiss.

He says, "It looks like we have more than enough for the market tonight."

Roscoe looks at Wold with big pleading eyes and says, "Daddy, can we get a goat? Mr. Allium has goats, and I love playing with them."

Wold groans. "No goats. Goats eat everything. Even more than the chickens, and I can barely stand them." I giggle at the thought of Wold having to drag a goat away from his mushrooms. As if on cue, our most cantankerous hen comes up and pecks at Wold's tail fur. He mutters darkly and tries to swat her away with his tail, but she is not deterred and pecks him again.

Roscoe says, "I got it Daddy." Wold sets him down and he screeches and flaps his arms and chases her away.

"Okay, Roscoe," I finally say, "it's nap time. You need to get rest for the market tonight."

Roscoe immediately starts grumbling.

"You don't want to fall asleep and miss everything again," I say.

He begrudgingly agrees and heads inside to his bedroom, walking as slowly as possible.

Wold gives me a heated look. I can see his eyes starting to glow brighter. He says, "I think we will take a nap too." I squeal when he scoops me up bridal style and carries me into the house.

Pampa is close enough for me to hear her groan and say, "Gross." I couldn't see her, but I'm sure there was epic eyerolling too.

When we get to our room, he brushes his hand on the wall to light up the mushrooms. As I watch all the mushrooms light up, I say, "That still hasn't gotten old."

He sets me on the bed and helps me tug my dress off.

I look up at him and say, "I missed you."

He smiles and says, "I missed you too."

He cradles my cheek in his palm, and he kisses me as he presses me back onto the bed and lays down between my thighs, resting his big body on mine. He buries his face between my breasts and inhales deeply. Then he sighs and says, "I will never get enough of this scent."

He buries his face between my breasts again as I idly stroke his hair.

"I love you, Wold."

He looks at me, his eyes glowing so brightly. "I love you too, Lydia. Forever."

"Forever," I agree.

The End

Lyra Lorne

KNOT WITHOUT

MY MATE

KNOT WITHOUT MY MATE

By Lyra Lorne

Chapter 1

I'M STILL IN THE kitchen when a hear a commotion coming from another part of the estate. With Lord Varik, this isn't unusual, so I continue thoroughly cleaning the kitchen and packing up a few items I need.

A few minutes later, one of the guards runs into the kitchen. He's out of breath and seems panicked. "It's Lord Varik. He's out of control. He has three guards glamoured and he's going to kill Faylen, Osonia, and the human woman! Everyone that is able needs to come help!"

My heart drops when he says Faylen. I grab my biggest cleaver and shout, "Where?"

As he runs down the hall, he yells, "The human's rooms! I'll get more guards."

I'm running before he can even finish his sentence. Not my Faylen.

From across the house, I hear glass shattering. No! I push myself to run faster. Not Faylen. Not my sweet Faylen. Please, Gods.

I hear fighting, and then a scream. Everything goes silent as I turn the corridor to the human's rooms. *Not Faylen. Not Faylen.* I chant this in time with my heartbeat.

I finally skid to a stop in the human's doorway. What I see is a blood bath. A Guardian is standing near the middle of the room, Lord Varik's body at his feet. Blood is everywhere. Osonia begins running for her male who is unconscious by a wall. My eyes dart over the room, searching for Faylen. I briefly note the human woman is standing beside the bed in a state of shock.

Then I find her. She has crumpled to her knees and she's holding her hands as if they hurt. My heart hammers in my chest as I look over her, trying to assess injuries. Then she looks up at me. Our eyes meet, and I say quietly, "Faylen, are you well?"

Tears are rolling down her cheeks and she shakes her head in answer to me. I stride across the room, pick her up, and carry her out of the room.

She leans against my chest and cries as I take her to her room.

When we get there, I see that her bag is mostly packed and waiting. I set her on the bed and sit down beside her. She's still cradling her hands to her chest. I gently say, "Faylen, let me see. What happened?" She sniffs and cries, but she allows me to gently pull her hands towards me.

I don't understand what I'm looking at. Her skin is stained gold. It covers her hands and wrists and moves partway up her arms.

"Faylen, what happened?"

She sniffles, then chokes out, "He used his powers to restrain us. He covered them in gold."

I look at her horrified. I'd heard rumors about the statues, but I always assumed that's what they were—just rumors.

She continues, "The gold melted off when he died, but now they look like this, and they feel numb and tingle. He did it to my feet, too."

She lifts her leg and pulls a boot off. Her feet are so delicate and small. I want to touch them, but I push that feeling away. I look at the skin—it's stained gold as well, although it's not as dark as her hands.

"Do they feel numb like your hands?"

She scrunches her forehead thinking about it. "They feel a little tingly, but not as bad as my hands. Maybe my boots helped protect them?"

"Maybe so. Let's get out of here. When we get to the nearest town, we will see a healer," I say.

She nods. "Thank you, Allium. Thank you for coming for me."

She looks at me with tears in her eyes, and my heart breaks. I cup her cheek. Her face looks so small and delicate compared to my massive hand and claws. "I should have come for you long ago. You never deserved anything he did to you."

She leans into my palm and sighs. She looks at peace and unafraid for once. She's looked afraid for so long, I've forgotten what she looks like when she's happy.

I say, "I'm sorry I didn't protect you, Faylen."

She smiles softly. "Don't feel guilty. I wouldn't have let you do anything that could have cost you your job."

I lean into her and kiss her soft lips.

FAYLEN

Chapter 2

My heart leapt when Allium came to save me. He came just to get me. When he picked me up and carried me out of there, it seemed like a dream.

Now he is kissing me. His lips aren't like mine. His top lip is split like a cat, and I've often wondered what it would be like to kiss him. It feels perfect. It doesn't feel awkward or strange. Even though our mouths are different, we still fit together.

I feel the slightest brush of his bumpy tongue as he encourages me to open for him, and I do. I drop all my fears and hesitations, all the worries I've ever had as an Elven about being with a Guardian. I let go of all of them as I fill our kiss with all my desire and longing and need. I press myself against him and cling to his neck as we desperately kiss each other. Our tongues tangle wildly as we try to devour each other. We both pour all of our pent-up longing and need into this.

He presses me back onto my bed and I wrap my legs around his waist, clinging to him.

His kisses leave my mouth and he makes his way down my neck and onto my shoulder. He's softly licking me with every kiss. Each brush of his mouth against my skin sparks a fire inside me.

I can't hold it back any longer, and I desperately begin pulling my skirts up. I whimper. "Allium, touch me...please." There is a soft rumble in his chest as he slides his fingers—his claws retracted—up the inside of my thigh and gently runs one through the folds of my pussy. I moan at the touch. He adds another finger and both easily glide through my pussy, betraying how wet I am. I've wanted him for so long. He circles his finger around my clit and I cry out.

Gasping, I say, "Allium, I need you inside me. Please."

He growls and rips his apron off. Then he hastily unbuttons his trousers and slides them down. His tail flicks wildly behind him, and he breathlessly says, "I can't knot you right now. We need to leave and that would take too long. But I can still fuck you."

My breath hitches. "You have a knot?"

He murmurs, "Yes. And you will love being stuck upon it, writhing is ecstasy as I pump you full of my seed."

I whimper and glance down as he spreads my legs far enough for his hips to fit between them. I've only ever had experience with Elven males, and Allium's cock is different than what I'm used to. The head is more tapered and pointed. Then below his cock head, his shaft bulges out slightly. That bulge is covered in textured bumps like his tongue. The bulge tapers back in slightly right before it flares out around what is becoming a huge, rounded knot.

Oh gods, that's his knot. He grips it tightly in his fist, then slicks the head of his cock through my pussy and finds my entrance. He slowly presses in and, gods, I didn't know a cock could feel this good. I can feel all the texture on it, and I moan loudly and grip onto his neck. I gasp and whimper as he thrusts into me slowly while still gripping his cock. After a few thrusts, he lets go of his knot and raises his chest off me as he begins to thrust harder. I can feel the knot hitting my pussy and stopping him from thrusting all the way in. He looks down and with a growl says, "It has swollen enough to stop me from knotting you. Now, I can fuck you the way I want to."

I whimper at his words. He pulls his hips back and thrusts into me hard. I cry out, "Fuck! Allium!"

He continues pounding into me hard, each thrust making me dizzy with pleasure. The texture on his cock and the feeling of his knot pressing against me pushes me closer and closer to an orgasm. I continue to moan loudly as he fucks me. When I feel right at the edge of coming, I slide my hand down and lightly graze my clit. That small touch is all it takes to push me over the edge, and I scream as my orgasm rips through me.

Allium moans and growls as I come, and then he yells as he thrusts into me one more time and he comes. He continues groaning as he spills his seed inside me in pulse after pulse of his cock.

He kisses me deeply as we lay entangled on the bed. "Faylen, I should have done this long ago."

I smile and kiss him again. When we finally break the kiss, he says, "We should leave now." I nod in agreement.

He pulls his cock out of me and grabs a towel. He helps me clean up, and we pack up the rest of my things.

***

As we leave, we stop by his room and the kitchen to get a few things he wanted to take with him. He doesn't have much, and he's able to add everything to my bag so it's easier to carry. As we pack up his things, he says, "We should be able to find work in the nearest town. I can cook and you can be a maid. And if the nearest town doesn't work out, we can try another. It might be hard at first, but we will be fine."

I nod and give him a smile. "Yes, I think you're right. We can figure this out together."

He clears his throat. "I've heard you speaking of wanting to open an inn someday. Maybe we can work towards that. I can cook, and you can tend to the rooms and the guests."

I smile and say, "That would be wonderful. I've always thought it was just a dream, and I would be trapped working for one wealthy aristocrat or another, but maybe we can make it work together."

He gives me a serious look. "No matter what happens, you will never need to work for anyone like that again."

Once we finish packing up, we go to the stables hoping to find a horse. Fortunately, all the horses were still here, along with both carts.

Allium chooses the strongest looking horse and saddles him for us.

As he's getting the horse ready, I see the silhouettes of Lydia and her Guardian coming toward the stable. Nanni and Pampa are with them!

"Allium, it's Nanni and Pampa! I'm going to say goodbye to them."

He looks past me to where I'm pointing. "Say your goodbyes. I'll finish getting the horse ready and come out there."

Chapter 3

I KEEP AN EYE on Faylen as she says goodbye to Nanni and Pampa. Even though I feel like she is safe, I am concerned that the human woman's Guardian might decide he wants revenge on his woman's behalf for how she was treated.

He shows no signs of hostility toward Faylen though, even when she speaks to the human woman and they embrace.

I am still relieved when she walks back towards me.

I help her onto the horse, then pull myself up behind her. I nod to the human woman's Guardian as we ride off.

As we leave the estate, I take the road to the right. Faylen finally speaks up. "Where are we going?"

I reply, "There is an inn not far from here. I think we should get a room for the night so you can rest. We can make a plan in the morning."

Faylen leans against me as we ride. I can tell she is exhausted, but I am also happy to notice that she is relaxed. Lately, Faylen has been more stressed and afraid every day. I could see the tension in her shoulders and jaw as she worked. She no longer smiled. I could even scent the anxiety and fear on her. I knew that he took her to his bed. I knew he was selfish and cruel, but Gods, I never imagined that he was everything the rumors said he was. Gods, I can't even imagine what she may have endured at his hands. I grit my teeth at the rage that burns inside me. All those nights that I knew she was with him; the only way it was bearable was if I told myself that she was getting pleasure. Now I realize how foolish that was. Of course he wasn't pleasing her. It was never about her. And now that I know how he really was...I wish I could have been the one to rip him apart. I unintentionally let out a low growl at the thought.

Faylen looks back at me. "Are you okay?"

"Sorry, I was just thinking about Lord Varik...I am glad he's gone."

She leans back against me and says, "Me too. It's like a weight has lifted off of me knowing that he can't hurt anyone now."

I lean down and kiss the top of her head. "I'm sorry, Faylen. If I had known..." I shift the reigns to my right hand and wrap my left arm around her and squeeze her close to me.

She rubs her hand over my arm. "Don't feel guilty. I didn't want you to know."

She goes quiet after that. After a few minutes, I feel her muscles start to tense. Soon I notice that her breathing is heavy. "Faylen, are you okay?"

She chokes on a sob and shakes her head, then she breaks down weeping. My arm is already tight around her, but I stop the horse, so I can hold her.

I stroke her hair out of her face and hold her. "It's okay, Faylen, you're safe. I have you." I wish that I could change what he did to her, but I can't, so I just hold her as she weeps. I stroke her hair, then I nuzzle my face into her neck. I continue to murmur to her that she's safe and that I have her. Eventually she stops weeping.

She sniffs. "I'm sorry Allium."

I stroke her hair out of the way and kiss her neck. "Don't be. I'm here for you. It will take time to heal those wounds. It doesn't matter how long it takes, I will be here for you."

She sniffs again and hiccups on her inhale, then she leans back against me. "Thank you, Allium."

I just hug her tightly to me. "Are you ready? We can stay here longer if you need."

She shakes her head. "I think I'm okay now."

We spend the rest of the journey quiet, lost in thought, and enjoying being close to one another.

***

When we arrive at the inn, I tie the horse to the post, then we go inside to speak to the innkeeper about a room and a stable for the horse.

He's a gruff older Guardian, and he has only one room left, but he has plenty of space in the stable. We take the room without question. After we pay, we take the horse around to the stable, then he shows us to our room.

Faylen quietly looks over the state of the room. It's not bad, especially for an inn, but it's not that good either. It's not really the type of place you want to take a female if you want to impress her.

It has a bed that looks soft and clean. There is also an attached bathing room with a decent sized tub in the middle of it. It's not big enough for a Guardian like me, but Faylen should fit in it nicely.

Before the innkeeper leaves, I say, "We would like water for a bath."

He grunts, "That'll be extra."

I nod and tell him I have the coin for it.

Once he leaves, Faylen sits down on the bed, lays back, and sighs. "The bed is actually pretty comfortable." Then she pushes herself up to rest on her elbows for a minute and studies me. "Thank you again, Allium. Thank you for helping me."

I walk to the edge of the bed, lean over, and cup her cheek. "I would always come for you."

She turns her head and kisses the palm of my hand. I lean in to kiss her, but there is a knock at the door, interrupting us. It's the innkeeper with a giant basin of water.

He takes it into the bathroom and pours it into the tub. Then he mutters, "I'll bring one more."

As he leaves the room to get the second basin of water, I sit down on the bed next to Faylen and take her hand. I rub my thumb over the skin on her palm, trying to fade the gold stain. "Do they still tingle?"

"Less than before. Do you think it's fading?" She gives me a worried look. It's not fading, and I can tell that she already knows that. This was just hope.

I don't want to disappoint her, but I can't lie to her. "No, I don't think so. We will find a healer in the morning and see what they can do."

She sighs in defeat, then she studies her hand while it's intwined with mine. "Well, at least it's pretty. It looks nice with my skin tone." She holds her hand out as if she's admiring it, then she gives me a tired smile. She takes a breath to say something else when the innkeeper walks back in.

He carries the water to the bathroom and pours it in the tub, then comes back into the room and collects the extra coin.

As he's leaving, he says, "You two have a g'night."

Once the door shuts, I turn to Faylen. "Come on, let's get you into the bath."

Chapter 4

ALLIUM LEADS ME INTO the bathroom. One glance at the water in the tub tells me that it's lukewarm at best, but I don't care. Soaking in any water would be nice right now.

Allium stands by the tub and looks at me expectantly. I should take my clothes off. I can't exactly bathe fully dressed. Suddenly though, I'm feeling shy. He didn't actually see all of me when we had sex, and the thought of being naked makes me feel so exposed.

Feeling exposed causes fear to suddenly slice into my chest. Lord Varik made me strip down in front of him like this. Mental images of the things he made me do suddenly flash through my mind. I can hear his cruel words ringing in my head. All his taunts and criticisms. All the pain and humiliation. All of it designed to tear me apart, both physically and mentally. All of it swirls together in my mind and I feel like I can't breathe.

My pulse pounds in my ears, and I feel like I'm gasping for air. All I can hear is Lord Varik's taunting voice echoing in my head. Allium must be able to sense my panic. He walks towards me and cups my cheek as he says, "Faylen, do you want me to go? I can wait in the bedroom."

I shake my head sharply, both to tell him no and to clear the memories. This is Allium. I don't have to be afraid of him. I'm safe.

I finally say, "No, I want you to stay."

He studies my face. "If you change your mind, tell me. I don't want you to be afraid. I know it might take some time."

"No, please stay. I'm not afraid of you."

I begin taking off my dress and underclothes and Allium steps back and watches me. Once my dress is off, I hand it to him. Then I quickly slip my underclothes off and hand them to him too.

"Can you lay those out on the bed for me?"

He nods, but his eyes are riveted to me and he doesn't move. I feel self-conscious for a moment, however I see that his eyes are drinking me in. I can tell from the bulge in his trousers that he likes what he sees. It gives me a little bit of confidence, and I stand up a little straighter and give him a small smile.

Then I walk over to the tub and step in. I was right, the water is barely warm, but it still feels so good as I sink down into it. I sigh as I settle in and relax.

I cast a glance back at Allium and he's still standing there staring at me, entranced, while holding my clothes. He has the most adorable look of wonder on his face.

I smile at that, then I laugh when I say, "Are you going to just stand there holding my clothes?"

He snaps out of his trance and slumps his shoulders a little bit in embarrassment before he says, "Oh...um...I'll just go lay these out."

I giggle a little as he walks out. Then I look around the bathroom, trying to find the soap.

Allium comes back a moment later, and I say, "Do you see soap?"

He looks around the small bathroom and sighs. "I bet we have to buy it." He lets out a frustrated little growl, and his tail flicks from side to side.

I quickly say, "Don't worry, I don't need it. I'm fine with just water."

He scoffs. "Give me a couple of minutes and I will get soap from the innkeeper. You stay here and relax."

I watch him walk out of the bathroom, tail still flicking, then I relax into the tub, lay my head back, and shut my eyes.

Chapter 5

My cock is hard and I'm irritated as I stalk downstairs to the innkeeper's desk. I hear my tail slap the wall as I go. He's working on some papers and gives me a questioning look when I walk up.

"Do you have soap?" I ask, more than a little annoyed that he didn't mention soap earlier.

He goes into a backroom behind the counter and comes back with a bar of soap. "I was wondering how long it would take you to come ask for this."

I scowl at him, and I can feel my tail flicking fiercely. "You couldn't mention it when you brought the water?" I hand him the coin for it and take the soap.

He chuckles in his throat and says, "You're just sore that you had to leave that female of yours alone in the tub."

Just as I'm about to turn to leave, he looks at me and says, "So how did someone like you end up with a sweet little Elven cunt like that?"

I give him a long look and let out a low growl.

He just chuckles, "Enjoy, brother." Then he goes back to whatever he was working on.

***

I growl as I storm back up the stairs. My tail angrily slaps the railing and the wall as I do. Of course he had to comment on her being Elven; he just couldn't help himself.

I'm about to open the door to the room when I realize that my anger won't help Faylen at all. She doesn't need me huffing and growling about a stupid comment some old innkeeper made. She's already dealing with enough fear from a bad male.

I sigh and scrub my hand down my face, then I force myself to take a few slow, deep breaths. Once I feel calmer, I open the door and go into our room.

From the bathroom, Faylen says, "Allium? Is that you?"

"Yes," I reply as I walk into the bathroom. I hand her the bar of soap. "I think that old innkeeper is trying to be difficult."

She just chuckles as she begins scrubbing her perfect opalescent orange skin. I lean against the wall and watch her. I'm losing myself in thoughts of her perfect skin and what it tastes like when I catch a glimpse of the gold staining on her hands. Well, perfect except for the marks he left on her. The gold would actually be very striking with her coloring, if it didn't have such a dark meaning.

She stands up to finish washing her body and the sight of her completely naked interrupts any other thoughts in my head. My tail slaps loudly against the door frame. She looks at me as she rubs the soap over her skin. "Allium, you okay?"

I pause for a moment, and my tail slaps loudly against the door frame again. I huff in embarrassment. "Yes, just...thinking."

"Do you think it will be hard to find work?"

Distracted, I say, "Hmm...no, finding a cooking job is easy. It just may not be a very nice one at first." I'm trying my hardest to hold a normal conversation with her—and keep my damn tail still—but all I can think about is how much I want to lick every inch of her. I can feel my cock straining against my trousers.

She nods. "It's like that as a maid too. It may not be fun or glamorous, but it will earn some coin."

By now she has scrubbed all over and she sits back down in the tub to rinse off. Once she's done, she stands back up and asks me to hand her a towel. I hand her the nearest one, and then I watch her intently as she dries off.

It's only then that I realize that her hair is dry and she's piled it on top of her head in a messy knot.

I foolishly say, "Your hair is dry."

She smiles at me and chuckles. "Yes, I know. I didn't want to take the time to wash it."

She folds the towel, hangs it over the side of the tub, and then walks straight toward me. She grabs my hand and begins pulling me into the bedroom.

As she does, she gives me a coy smile and says, "Come."

FAYLEN

Chapter 6

I'm not a fool. I knew Allium was watching me. I knew what he was thinking about.

After I'm finished bathing, while still completely naked, I lead him into the bedroom. I sit down on the edge of the bed and then reach up and begin unbuttoning each of the buttons on his trousers. He takes a ragged breath as I do, and his tail thrashes wildly.

His cock is already hard and straining against his trousers. With each button I undo, I see a little more of it. Once his trousers are completely unbuttoned, his cock falls free of its restraint, and I begin sliding his trousers down his hips. He takes over and slides them completely off.

Then he's standing before me, completely naked, cock hard and leaking a bead of precum. I reach a hand out and run my fingers along the length of his shaft. He groans as I touch him. His cock is so much different than any I've seen before. I run my fingers over those delicious bumps. When I reach his knot, I wrap my hand around it. I can feel it swelling just from my touch. Then I lean forward and lick the precum off the head of his cock.

He gasps and groans, then breathlessly says, "Faylen, if you keep doing that, it will swell too much." He lets out another little groan, "And I want to knot you tonight."

I feel my pussy clench when he says that. "You do?"

He growls, "Yes, I want to knot you and fill you will my seed so that your belly will be swollen with my cubs soon."

I gasp. "You want that?"

He growls and leans down to kiss me. Then he breathes his next words against my lips. "You are mine now, Faylen, and I intend to breed you every chance I get."

I shudder at his words, then whimper as he begins to press me back onto the bed. He kisses and licks down my neck as his fingers slide over my pussy. He presses a finger into me, and I moan because his touch feels so good. I gasp as his finger finds that perfect spot on the inside of my pussy. He continues to work his finger inside me, and I can hear the slick, wet sounds that my body is making. Then he presses a second finger inside me and, oh gods, his fingers are so thick. I moan as he fucks me with them. I feel him spreading his fingers apart, stretching me. I whine and pant while I cling to him as he does this. Impossibly, he begins to press a third thick finger into me. I whimper at the intensity of him stretching me, but it feels so good.

Allium whispers, "Good girl. You are opening up for me so well." I whimper at his words, then I feel him beginning to spread his fingers and I nearly cry out at how intense it is. I feel impossibly full. I writhe and squirm against the pressure.

Allium says, "Shhhh. You are doing so good. I need to make sure you are nice and open so you can take my knot."

Allium rotates his hand and brushes his thumb against my clit, and I cry out. "Fuck, Alli...do that again."

He growls into my neck, then he begins rubbing his thumb in a light circle over my clit, and I cry out. He spreads his fingers more inside me, stretching me even more. I whimper and writhe against him. It's so much, but so good all at the same time.

I feel the pleasure building in my belly, and I know I'm going to come soon. My legs start to tremble.

Allium groans and says, "Good girl, Faylen, you are going to take my knot so well. Come for me and show me how much you want it."

That's all it takes. Pleasure crashes over me, and I cry out as I come. My pussy pulses around his fingers, and Allium growls as he buries his face in my neck.

I'm breathless as my orgasm subsides, but I still need more. I need him. I need him inside me.

I manage to say, "Alli, make me yours, knot me...please."

He growls and it becomes a long groan. He slides his hips between my legs and slicks his cock through my pussy, notching it at my entrance. Then he slowly begins pressing into me. I cry out loudly as he does.

I feel that first swell and all those bumps as he thrusts into me, then I feel his knot pressing against me. He pulls almost all the way out, then thrusts back into me again. I feel delicious pressure as his knot begins pressing into me. I can already feel the stretch, and it's only just starting to enter me. I cry out as I stretch more around it as he slowly thrusts into me. He pauses to see if I'm okay, but I take a ragged breath and say, "Don't stop, please, don't stop. Gods, Alli, it's so good."

He growls against my throat, and I feel the slight brush of his sharp fangs as he begins to slowly thrust into me again. His knot continues to stretch me while I whine and dig my nails into his back. Just when I feel like it's too much, and I can't possibly take anymore, his cock slides all the way in and I feel his hips press against mine. My pussy closes and grips tightly around his knot. We are both breathless. I can still feel it swelling even more inside me. I'm stretched so much, but it feels so good.

He tries to shift his hips back and thrust back into me, but I am knotted to him and his swollen cock barely moves inside me. With me locked onto him, every small movement of his hips sends a wave of pleasure through me and I can feel my pussy pulse around him every time he moves.

He groans loudly with each movement. I can feel his muscles beginning to tighten and tremble, and I know he's going to come soon, so I whisper, "Alli, let me ride you."

His breath hitches, then he begins shifting and rolling us over so that I am on top of him, straddling his hips.

I grind my pussy down on him, and he nearly yells with the pleasure of it. I moan and gasp as I grind against him. It feels so good. His knot is pressing against everything inside me, and grinding against him puts pressure on all the right places. I can feel the pleasure building inside me.

I grind harder against him, building that pleasure even higher. Both of us are moaning loudly now. I lean forward and grab his horns. I pull his face to look at me and breathlessly say, "Alli, make me yours. Fill me with your seed and your cubs."

He growls loudly then grabs me by the hips and presses me against him as he thrusts into me. I moan with pleasure and then scream as my orgasm tears through me. My pussy, stuffed so full, flutters around his cock.

He shudders in the next breath and roars as he comes. I can feel his cock pulsing inside me as he fills me with seed.

I collapse forward onto his chest, both of us breathing heavily. I try to shift my hips slightly and feel the pull of his knot still swollen inside me.

I must give him a look of surprise because he chuckles and says, "It will stay like that for a while. I'll have to fill you at least one more time before it will go down."

I gasp. "Really?"

He just chuckles again. "Rest for now."

I lay my head back on his chest and just let my body relax for the first time in a long time. I run my fingers through the fur on his chest and absently play with it. Everything feels so peaceful, so right.

After a few minutes I say, "Allium, what is the plan for tomorrow?"

He growls low in his throat then says, "More of this."

I laugh and he grunts as my muscles reflexively tighten around his cock. "And after that?" I say coyly.

He growls softly, "Maybe even more of this." Then he lightly thrusts his hips into me. The slight movement of his knot inside me makes me gasp softly.

I can hear the huskiness in my voice when I say, "At some point we have to get out of this bed, then what?"

He thrusts into me again, a little harder this time, and I moan and grind myself against him.

He continues to thrust into me and says, "We will go to the city. Find a healer and find...." He groans loudly. Then he tries to pick up what he was saying, "Find...find... Fuck, Faylen..." He groans again.

At this point, I don't even care what he says we are doing. He could have said we are going to the moon and I would have been fine with it. All I can focus on is his cock inside me, and how good it feels.

He pulls me to his chest and then rolls us over so he is on top of me. Because of his knot, his thrusts are short, but he's thrusting into me faster now and grinding against me. I cry out with each thrust. Then I grab his horns and pull his face towards me and nip at his lower lip. I hear a rumble deep in his throat, then he crushes his mouth against mine and kisses me deeply. I'm breathless and clinging to his horns by the time he pulls his mouth from mine.

He buries his face in my neck and I feel the brush of his sharp teeth. Then he growls and says in a husky voice,

"Faylen, is this what you want? To be my mate? To be mated to a Guardian?"

My breath hitches. "Yes Allium, I want to be your mate."

He brushes his teeth against my neck again, then I feel his tail slide between us to brush against my clit. Just as I moan from pleasure, he sinks his teeth into my neck, biting me. I had forgotten about Guardian mating bites, so I cry out in surprise. There is only a moment of sharp pain, then all I feel is warm tingling pleasure. It fuels the pleasure that is building low in my belly and suddenly that pleasure explodes through me. Allium has me pinned in place with his teeth and his cock, but I writhe against him as I come. It's only a matter of moments before he growls loudly into my neck as he comes.

Once we have both come down from our orgasms, he carefully pulls his teeth out of my skin and gently licks the small wounds left behind. Then he kisses me deeply.

I can feel his knot getting smaller inside me, and several long, peaceful minutes later, he is able to shift off me and lay down beside me. I gasp as I feel a flood of seed seep out of me. Allium laughs, and gets up to grab a towel, then he helps me clean up.

Once he is back in bed, I snuggle up to his chest. I begin running my fingers through his fur again, and it's then that

I notice that some of the gold on my hands and arms has faded. It's darker at my fingertips and gets lighter on my palm, but by my wrist it is faded away completely. It also doesn't tingle anymore.

"Alli, look," I say excitedly. I hold out my hands.

Then I notice on my arms that I have faintly darker markings. They look like Allium's markings. I gasp as I realize that it runs up my arms, onto my torso, and all the way down my legs.

I give Allium a wide-eyed look. "They are markings like yours!"

He touches one and rubs his finger over it. He has a look of wonder on his face. He finally looks up at me and says, "It must have been my mating bite. I didn't know…" His look suddenly darkens as he says, "I'm sorry, Faylen, I didn't realize it would do this."

I laugh as I say, "No, Alli, I'm not mad. I love it." Then I grab his face and kiss him.

Once we finally stop kissing, we snuggle up to each other. I graze my hand over my belly. "I wonder how long it will take for me to get pregnant. What if I'm already pregnant?"

He chuckles, "Don't worry, I intend to knot you a lot to make sure you are pregnant soon." He kisses me again. "Get some sleep. You need your rest."

I kiss him lightly on the lips. "Goodnight, Allium." Then I drift off into peaceful sleep.

***

We end up staying at the inn for two more days. We spend all of it in bed, except for when Allium goes downstairs to get us food and pay the innkeeper.

On our second night there, I jolt awake after a horrible nightmare about Lord Varik. Allium wakes up with me and holds me while I sob into his chest. He's so patient with me as he helps me, I couldn't ask for a better mate. I eventually cry myself back to sleep while he holds me and whispers soothing reassurances. When I wake up the next morning, he's asleep but still holding me.

Once we finally decide it's time to leave the bed, we both need a bath. Allium tells me to take mine first, then he attempts to take one himself. He hilariously does not fit in the tub. His legs and arms hang out, and half the water ends up on the floor. Finally, he decides to just stand in the tub and use a cloth to wash up. By the end of it, he looks like a grumpy barn cat that's been stuck in the rain. Despite all my giggling, I try to help him dry his fur, although that just ends with us in bed again.

Later that day, we pack up and leave on our horse, heading toward the city. Our plan is to find a healer and a place to stay.

I lean back against Allium and rest my head on his chest as we peacefully ride toward our new life. I lightly rub my hand over my belly. I have every intention of asking that healer if I'm pregnant, but I think I already know the answer.

In the distance, I'm beginning to be able to see the buildings of Lamrione, and I realize that for the first time in a very long time, I feel completely happy and excited for the future.

FAYLEN

Epilogue

1 year later

The babies start crying well before the sun comes up. Allium groans and rolls away from where we are snuggling together and picks up one of them. I hear him changing the baby's diaper cloth, then he brings the baby to me in bed so I can nurse him. He then picks up the other crying baby and changes his diaper cloth before bringing him to me as well.

I have a baby nursing on each breast and I'm so tired that it aches, but I have never been so happy as I am now.

Allium is the perfect mate and father, just as I knew he would be.

We've recently purchased an older inn and tavern on the outskirts of our realm, very near to the human world. It belonged to one of Allium's distant uncles. He was getting older and was tired of running the place, so we purchased it and moved in just before the twins were born.

The inn needs a lot of repairs, so Allium has spent his days working on that. Two of his younger brothers are staying with us to help with the repairs.

Allium has a huge family with many brothers and sisters. Apparently, it's customary in the mountains where he's from that the oldest son takes over Guardian duties of their family's territory. The rest of the children are expected to learn skills and move out into the world and make lives for themselves. Allium chose to learn to cook. His two younger brothers are carpenters and have been so helpful with the repairs. I don't know how we would have done it without them.

It's been wonderful having them stay with us.

I was an only child growing up, and my parents didn't pay much attention to me, so I've never known what it was like to have a real family.

I love seeing Allium with his brothers, and I am so glad that my boys will be able to have that kind of bond as well.

Apparently, Allium's people like to have a lot of babies. In fact, Allium had already started talking about more babies recently, but I've convinced him to wait a few years.

I want plenty of time to spend with the twins before I must divide my attention between them and a new baby, or two.

I try not to think about Lord Varik anymore. I had nightmares for a while, and crying fits during the day, but Allium has helped me work through a lot of what happened. Sometimes now there are several days that I don't think about it at all. I know it's getting better, and hopefully someday soon, I will never think of him again.

My fingertips and toes are still the same gold that they were the night Allium gave me his mating bite, but it doesn't bother me anymore. I like the way it looks, especially the way it contrasts with the markings from Allium's mating bite. I made hand puppets out of some of the golden fabric from the clothes I took from Lord Varik's estate. I make up little stories and sing songs for the boys with the puppets. I know they are still babies, but I like to think that one day, the boys will just see the gold on my fingers as the magic from my stories.

There is one thing I am grateful to Lord Varik for, though. If it hadn't been for working at his horrible estate, I never would have met Allium. I would relive all of that pain again and again, just to be with my mate.

The End

ACKNOWLEDGEMENTS

Thank you to everyone that has helped me dream this book to life. Every person that has played a part in this, including every Instagram like and Patreon membership means the world to me.

A special thank you to Lianne for creating Lydia and Wold as a sketch. And thank you for the endless support, encouragement, and sketches.

Thank you to my awesome husband who always believes in me and is willing to help me with any dream I have.

Thank you to my editor, YarnWyvern, for all the hard work and funny comments.

And thank you to my PA, Jessie, for helping me keep my ADHD ducks in a row.

When Lyra Lorne isn't daydreaming or writing, she can be found hiding from the heat in the sprawling suburbs of Texas. She enjoys spending time with her family and menagerie of pets and doing anything creative.

For sneak peeks into current projects and exclusive artwork visit www.lyralorne.com.